To my dance family
Who always believed that a person can do anything
So long as they put in enough hard work.

Index

Sleisia: the country- An empire run by an Emperor and Empress
Oslia: the military
Oswana: city the Military trains in
Kheross: city the Capital is located.
Sloeq Plan: the biggest prison in Sleisia

Order of Training levels for an Oslian Soldier:
Kuswax: Beginning entry level as part of Oslia (5-6 years of age)
Juspan
Asmye
Othla
Truji
Swaejan: level right before graduating (20 years old)

Ranking in the Country of Sleisia
Paramount: Government officials, Soldiers, officials, and the leaders
Bemoura: middle class that does pointless jobs
Infective: they serve everyone that is above them, they are dirt poor **Infinitive**: they have been completely

forgotten about by Sleisia, they're either homeless or on the verge of banishment

Victor's house to Sloeq Plan: the Victor's house is a good distance from the prison and Victor's must walk in a stretch of desert each day from the house to the prison.

Chapter One

I try to smooth out my silky, white dress one last time before I leave the room. I stare into the long, floor length mirror one last time, feeling like one of the government superiors for the first time in my life. I have never worn something as extravagant as this. Behind me someone sighs and I turn to face the people standing with me outside the church.

My friend Maria clasps my hands in between the both of us. "Jason is one lucky guy." I smile at her, a slight blush warming my cheeks.

She does a full circle around me, double checking any loose hairs or ribbons. When she's satisfied that everything is in place she stands back with the rest of our friends so that they can survey me.

"Today's festivities makes it almost feel like the raids aren't going on,"Camilia, my cousin's wife, comments.

The smile on my face falters at the mention of the raids. The raids are a horrible travesty that the empire of Sleisia has unleashed on the world. For now the raids are only destroying the soldiers servants, the people who Sleisia thinks below them. As their leaders try to get a tighter grip on this country, they destroy all that is good and beautiful. The Oslia soldiers kill and destroy in these raids… only a few prisoners are taken, sometimes none at all. What they do with these prisoners has never been known. You can only hear their screams as the Oslia trucks drive through your province.

I try, again, to gain my smooth composure… pushing away all of the tarnished thoughts about the raids passing through my head. I take a few calming breaths as my friends gather up the wildflower bouquets that we picked earlier this morning. Soon, the doors are opening and I can hear Sebastian playing the church's piano before I can even see inside. My heart races, I can hear its beats in my ears. I watch first as Camilia, Sofia, and then Maria walk down the short aisle before taking a seat at the front of the church; then it's my turn. As soon as I enter the vast hall, I can see his face. Every chiseled outline is framed by his dark brown hair that hides the thin scar that I know runs across his forehead. Within seconds I know that I'll be up on the altar and then I'll be able to stare into his stormy colored eyes. But all of my past fears slowly drift away as each step that gets me closer to him. When I reach the altar he takes my hands in his, softly rubbing at the calluses that mark up my hands from years of work. Just as about the happiest day of my life is about to unfold, the back doors of the church burst open.

I only have enough time to turn around and get my first glance at the Oslian soldiers before the first shots are fired. Shock and chaos fills the room as people scream and run to take cover but I'm the only one who can't will their feet to move. A body suddenly flies at me and I am soon tackled to the ground. I sit up quickly in a hope to view the disaster that is taking place in the church but a muffled moan sounds from behind me. Jason lays, face down, on the ground, moaning in pain. I crawl on my hands and knees, helplessly, so that I may reach him. I flip his body over and pull him into my arms as sobs rack through my body. There's so much blood. Shots fired throughout the room and people drop like rocks but all I can do is cry as my dying fiancé bleeds out all over me. I flick my eyes up at the rest of the room to see soldiers rushing at me. When I look down at Jason's face life has completely bled from it and his eyes have slid shut. My mouth slips open and an endless line of screams escapes from my lips and then the first hands reach me.

Several more Oslians reach us and start to pull me away from my dead husband; I scream, cry, and kick, hoping to hit anything that gets close enough. I try as hard as I can to fight my way out of their grasp but I'm getting weak from each slap, punch, and kick that I receive from trying to fight. They drag me all the way out of the church and throw me into the back of one of their trucks. The doors slam shut behind me and the floor starts to rock from underneath my body. I look around at the back of the truck and find only one prisoner. Me.

As soon as the truck stops I am blindfolded and thrown into a steel cold cell. I wait crumbled there for hours, chained against the back wall in a crumble. The cell's door swings open on rusty hinges after hours of me sitting there. Rough, cold hands grab at each side of my face, pulling off the blindfold. Before me stands a black haired, giant of a man, there's a sly smile on his face as he pinches a strand of my brown hair between his fingers. I try to scramble away but I can't.

"Oh, come on," He breathes as one of his hands moves to caress my cheek. "Don't be like that, bebe," He whispers in my language.

A whimper escapes from my lips when his face comes within inches of mine.

"Leave the prisoner alone, Bryan," A new Oslian Soldier commands the man cupping my cheek. "Just go wait in the hall," The soldier lets go of me and starts to leave but not before he slaps me across the face.

I shrink against the wall as the new guy approaches me. "You're Kieranna Alejanero and you're 20 years old," The Oslian soldier stays a few feet away from me down in a crouched position and I have to resist the urge to ask whether that is a question or not. I nod my head really quickly so that he can't see my fear. "Put these on," He commands throwing a black wad at me that appears to be a soldier's uniform, only this one is made to fit a woman's figure.

The soldier comes closer to me and just when I think he's about to strike, he unlocks me from my chains. I cower against the wall, still too frightened to move, all the while rubbing my blistered wrists. The Oslian soldier walks to the door and turns around when he notices that I haven't moved to change into the uniform.

"You can either put it on or I can have Bryan come back in here and do it for you!"

As soon as the door shuts I quickly strip out of my blood stained dress and change into these thin black garments before Bryan comes back. I stand with my back pressed flat against the back concrete wall dressed in a tight black top and thin, stretchy black pants but they look somewhat like the jeans I were back at home. I tie up the knee high boots and then pull my hair back into its long ponytail. The door to my cell once again flies open and I am pulled from that dank place, getting one last look at my white and red dress. I am pulled through small, concrete hallways until I am led to a completely different room where I am laid down on a table with an I.V. stuck in my arm. Just about the time that some drug has started to seep into my veins, a whole new man shows up. The new man passes a feeling of importance through me when I have to watch as he commands the room about us. Machines are soon positioned above my head and I start to squirm as a sleeping drug is inserted into the drip that leads to my veins.

"Well Miss Alejandero. This machine above you," The official looking man says, patting the metal contraption above me. "Will insert itself into your brain so that we can take your current memories and replace them with more appropriate ones for an Oslian soldier."

The things the man says makes absolutely no sense- there is no way that you can actually take someone's memories. "Shall we begin?" I drift off to sleep just as the sound of a drill surrounds me.

I wake up in my room back at the Oslian training center back in Oswaina but as soon as I sit up I know something is wrong. I'm still wearing my black training uniform from the day before and a deep ache is within my skull. My fingers graze up at the top of my head where a long jagged scar is hidden behind all of my hair that I can't even remember getting it but the most unsettling thing is that none of my thoughts feel like my own. Something feels off. I can remember things like I would any other day but it feels like someone's feeding me these facts instead of actually me remembering them.

I know without a doubt that I am the first woman in the history of all Sleisia, to be an Oslain soldier. I live in the province of Esmana, one of the richest. This province in mainly inhabited by soldiers and government officials. I know with absolute certainty that I am currently at the main Oslian training center, in the province of Oswaina. I will soon be graduating at the top of my class, giving me many enemies seeing as the ranking in which we will graduate does impact the assignment that we get later on in life.

Somethings are far more certain; not all things feel foreign to my scrambled mind. I am Kiera Pole. Twenty-one years old and I grew up in Oslia-Oswaina. I was taken from my family at six years old. The entirety of my family is dead. I don't even remember where they are buried. Both of my older brothers died in combat when I was seven and my father was killed by the rebel group that tends to infect our streets. My mother. My poor mother died hours after I was born. At some point after that I was placed in the Academy where they've trained, fed and raised me since.

There's really a basic chain of hierarchy that each and every soldier goes through. Right away you come in as a Kuswax (the lowest of the low, but then again you're only a Kuswax from age six to ten), you jump up to being a Juspon but that's only a couple years, then Asmye, Othla, Truji, and finally graduating as a Swaejan just like I am currently. It was until I was a Truji that I was finally able to leave Oslia for the first time that I can remember. By that point I was eighteen. Although I now live in Esmana, I am required to go back to Oslia for training every day.

Even if the plainest of plain facts do make sense, others do not. My first raid for instance is a complete blur of confusion. A church way back when I was a Asmye, was having a wedding. Any young Asmye is always in charge of driving the truck for their first raid. Which you know is alright except for the fact that no one has the slightest clue for the purpose of it but one was never expected. Oslain soldiers don't expect one; we just do as we are told. I know nothing about that day. No one truly does. Plenty of rumors are said but who can say a single one holds any truth. Supposedly two people were taken. A man and a woman. The bride and the groom. It's troubling sure but I can't discern why.

Chapter Two

"Hey, Kier," A sharp hiss echos in my ear drum.

I take my eye away from the scope on my rifle and snap the word "What?" rather sharply right into my friend's, Christopher's, face.

My blood boils, beyond enraged that he has the guts to talk during a raid. Both of my eyes snap back to the house we have been surveying for the last half hour, now pissed at myself for giving him a fraction of a second of my attention. The only thing that should have my full attention right now is the current raid at hand and awaiting the orders to attack.

"There's a rumor going around the academy that the duration of our last three weeks of training, four Swaejan will be selected to go to Sloeq Plan for special training," both him and his excitement bump right into me, causing me to loose my mark. "They're supposed to be running the entirety of the prison."

I straighten up slightly… just the thought of being head of the most feared prison sends chills of excitement through me. Just being able to work in Sloeq Plan for a short period of time could really rocket my career forward. My head spins at the possibilities but I must force myself to snap out of my indulgence. This is a raid. It is time to focus. Oslian Soldiers do not daydream.

"Well, at this rate it won't be you. You can't shut your big mouth long enough to focus," I snap, annoyed with him and with myself.

I'm not given much more chance to scold him, even though I'd greatly like to; our commanding officer has finally given us our first orders in hours. The both of us spring up from our crouched position, ignoring any ache in our sore joints, and move almost cat like to hug along the wall of the house we've been sitting outside. Everyone files in a single line through the very narrow doorway, every single weapon trained at every possible position, making sure not to miss an inch of space. With a flick of my two first fingers Chris steps in front of me, his gun trained on the small hallway ahead of us. There's only one door at the end of the hall. There's no point in breaking down the door, as soon as Chris knows I'm ready he twists the door knob and flings the door open.

Just inside the door sit two people, huddled in the fake porcelain bathtub. Chris is able to get them into cuffs easily and within seconds; regrettably, the other man is not so compliant. When I try to even get near him he fights with I'm sure is everything he has. He has viscously groomed nails that he uses to try and claw at me through the air. I have no choice but to grab the top of his head and pull him along after me by the roots of his hair. I drag him along, out into the hallway all the while his body is bent down by my ankles as his hair is ripped from his head. The boy who barely could qualify as a man has no choice but to slink along and follow my commands like a dog who knows he's in trouble.

I shoved him down roughly onto his knees next to the rest of the prisoners and I am able to cuff his wrists together with two round metal circles. He stays there whimpering pathetically and his cries only intensify when I place the round, spherical opening of my gun against the nape of his neck. Every single one us, soldiers, wait with our eyes faced forward not moving. Not communicating with one another. I can almost feel the air around me when Chris shifts his position slightly as his muscles start to tire from standing still for so long. While we wait I focus on all the details of the dirt clinging to the dingy house. A round table maybe only meant for four people has at least six chairs crowded around it on the once blue, but now faded to grey, carpet. Something about this place's simplicity fills my heart with a deep sadness.

After an appropriate amount of time our commanding officer holds up a single finger. From the noise that follows after would cause any person to think that hell has broken out inside the rundown house. Several guns are fired all at once while screams erupt as those who have not yet fallen witness their friends drop to the floor, their eyes lifeless. When it's my turn, I don't hesitate, I pull the trigger without feeling any empathy. I don't even look over at Christopher when the deed is done. The procession of killings is soon over and we all break rank to file back out of the house and the clean up crew can come dispose of the bodies. As we file back out of the house in a little line I can't help but notice that Bryan still grasps hold of his prisoner. I was not aware that any one was going to be taken; he must have received a private command before me left or just moments early through his ear piece.

Outside I gulp in the cool air, glad to finally be free of the smell of death and blood. I linger far behind everyone else as they pile into the truck and watch as Bryan practically throws the boy who couldn't be any older than I am, into the back of one of the trucks and locks him in. Part of me can't help but sympathize with him, those metal floors are cold.

I shove all of my own personal weapons and leather armoring into my duffle, slightly irritated with my day right now and I don't even know why. I don't even get the chance to make my escape though because Christopher comes in. The possibility of getting back to my dwelling in Esmana seems smaller and smaller every second.

"You want to get some dinner?" He asks, leaning back against the wall, he's the most color that these bland dorm walls have ever seen.

"Why?" I can't help but sound slightly disgruntled by this idea, it is beyond confusing as to why he'd want to go out on a raid night.

Every single night that there is a raid the soldiers that partake in it have to fill out a report for their own training files. Every action that a soldier makes must be recorded. Over time a massive file will be built up of all of the raids and battles that a soldier has participated in. These files help earn higher positions in the military but these files can also be accessed when a soldier dies. That way all of Sleisia can see what a loyal soldier that particular diseased has been.

"I just need a brief break. We've been worked so hard lately that at the moment I just can't take it," I look at Christopher with a very weary gaze, it's very rare to hear him complain about anything Oslia does.

"Alright. I guess that would be fine," I begrudgingly reply.

"Excellent!" He grunts and I get a glimpse of my Chris underneath this non-compliant exterior. "We're going," he states.

There's no discussion. There's no talking about it. He states it plain and simple. He even asks questions similarly at times.

Our meal feels utterly excruciating. It takes forever to simply get our order in. It's not as if we weren't seated right away, being soldiers, we got our pick of the tables but as every second ticks by all I can think of is the thought of getting my report done. Even little small-talk from Chris can not keep me interested. I have my whole report basically mapped out inside my head before our food even comes.

Finally my peppered chicken comes and I dig my knife into the meat, hoping to get through this meal as quickly as possible. I'm several bites in to my meal but Chris has yet to even pick up his fork and knife.

"Kier?" He asks almost timidly. "Do you remember our first raid?"

"Of course I do," I say leaning back… taking a sip of water, trying to remember that day. "It was on a church."

He looks at me almost with a look of concern. "What do you remember about it?"

I'm more than slightly confused when I answer, "I drove one of the trucks."

I try to shrug it off and take another bite of my food but Chris catches hold of my wrist, stopping me.

I roll my eyes at him. "So, you don't remember specific details about that day?"

"I remember," I say then pause, trying to reflect back on that day and sort through the grey murk in my brain to reach that particular memory. "Two prisoners were taken that day: the bride and the groom."

"Yes!" He exclaims rather excitedly and more than a few disapproving eyes look over at us.

I fix him with a rather puzzled look; I have long since ignored the weird feeling I get whenever I think about that day. When I brought that feeling up with Chris, he told me I was delusional and walked away from me. So now it surprises me that he'd bring such a thing up now.

"Yeah. Well…" he almost bounces with excitement. "I heard something interesting yesterday. About that raid. Bryan told me," he stops just long enough to let me get in a disgusted noise before continuing. "That while the bride may be dead, the groom is alive. He's being held in one of our most secure prisons."

The corners of my lips stray to curl up on reflex. I should have known he'd want to talk about this sooner rather than later. "I know why you wanted to come here," I say, half tempted to reach out and pat his hand.

"You do?" He asks, almost turning sheepish again.

"Yes," I breath, my heart slightly skipping a beat. "You want to talk about Sloeq Plan," his mouth falls ever so slightly agape and I realize that we are being very unprofessional and I feel like clearing that up. "As your friend I won't report you for talking during a raid. Just don't let it happen again."

There are many things that a person is not allowed to do during a raid and talking is one of them. It causes a distraction from the task at hand. If commandment was to ever find out then it would be taken out on your back in the form of whippings. There are six members of commandment, each incharge of a different training level but the higher up you get the more likely you are to get a citation. A citation basically cuts you down a rank, it can affect what job you get or just later on in life. There are basically four levels of ranking in our country: Paramount (Government officials, Soldiers, officials, and the leaders), Bemoura (middle class that does pointless jobs), Infective (they serve everyone that is above them, they are dirt poor) and the Infinitive (they have been completely forgotten about by Sleisia, they're either homeless or on the verge of banishment).

"No," he says a little too loudly and people once again look at us. "That's not why I wanted you to come with me tonight."

"It's alright. Even if they did give you a citation, that doesn't mean that they'll make you an Infective right away," I take a drink of my water and think of what it would be like to get those three citations needed to become an Infective.

But, when I look up at him again, I can tell that there's a hurt in his eyes and I automatically know that I was wrong. I've hit a nerve that I should have foreseen. Christopher's own brother got enough citations to be demoted to Infective; there was even a rumor going round that he was even demoted to Infinitive for a while, practically on the verge of being banished to the out skirt desert.

"You didn't want to talk about Sloeq Plan, you wanted to talk about your brother?" I almost feel ashamed for saying it.

My face is beet red and I take a sip of my water in an attempt to cool my face's temperature down a few degrees.

"There's a new rumor going around that he might be a prisoner somewhere," He looks kind of sad admitting this to me.

Several of the rumors included his brother being made an Infinite but only one that I know of actually involved him being banished; no one even knows for sure what his first citation was for. Apparently he was sacrificed to the desert outside our borders. No. I think that there's no way he would have been that dumb enough to do anything worthy of being banished. His brother would have had to have more pride than that. He has to be out there, rotting away in some alley with the other homeless. Supposedly, he's even tried to reach out to Christopher over the last couple years but I've never once known him to reply. Many years ago, I can just barely remember what it was like for him to walk our training campus but a clear image of him refuses to solidify in my mind.

"Look," I say and try to clear whatever is left in my throat. "I apologize for mentioning the Infective like that. Why don't you tell me about Sloeq Plan?"

I try and say in an attempt to distract him. When seconds ago there was a frown, so deep that I feared I had actually hurt him in a very personal way, there is the utmost excited look that could only be described as something a puppy would look like. Christopher is so bipolar sometimes that it almost frightens me. Part of me has a flashing memory of the back of his hand raised, about to strike my cheek but it's fleeting and only there for a few seconds. All I can do is guess that it was back when we were children and he didn't have his mood swings quite in check.

"There's supposed to be an official announcement tomorrow," When he says this his voice sounds as giddy as a child's, warning me once again of the ever changing moves of his emotions. "Supposedly, two jobs will be offered from this training. As soon as our class graduates, two of us will have the most high ranking jobs in history of someone at our age. Someone will even end up as the new Head Commander over Sloeq Plan."

It's hard for my mind not to boggle over this idea of being Commander of our biggest prison. It took the last guy at least thirty years and he was a mean, old bastard who had every right to be feared.

"The government themselves will be evaluating those chosen," He continues to say.

"Well what's the second position?" I can't help but ask, my curiosity getting the best of me.

The grin on his face is so very big that I can almost forget about the mournful look that was on his face moments ago, but not quite.

"When the emperor's son takes over, he needs a right hand man to take over," I almost blurt out the word 'woman' over his answer to me. "So he gets to choose out of the top four of our class. And what's better than having a well trained soldier working beside you, protecting you for the rest of your life?"

The whole thing sounds pretty spectacular but to those few who actually end up participating must have some sort of silver lining, the whole thing must be to good to be true.

"And what will happen to the other two chosen?" My brain can't seem to come up with what punishment Oslia will come up with for those who fail.

There's a slight sigh in his throat, his mood changing slightly again when he responds bluntly, "They will be banished."

Chapter Three

I walk into the vast room and am immediately assaulted by the smell of boys. There are many perks to being the first and only woman in our military but dealing with all of the boys stench is not part of it. I push and shove past all those of lower rank than me and allow myself to wiggle my nose at those who serve the grey slop that somehow passes for food that plops down on my plate. A half formed snarl sits in my throat as I make my way to a table that my friends occupy. Two boys sit at the table that I normally occupy, they don't even look up when I sit down across from them. They are both shoveling in the mounds of food laid out before them, as if it were the best thing they ever tasted.

I can't help but notice that Christopher is nowhere to be seen in the room, it was only yesterday that we had our last conversation and we haven't spoken to each other since. My eyes flit around the room hoping to catch a glimpse of him; it's odd that he's not here already, sitting with us.

"What's she looking for?" Val asks aloud and I know that he's just asking our other friend Lea but I can't help but take a slight interest in them, after all they are now talking about me.

"She's looking for Chris you nimrod," Lea's obviously fed up with Val by this point in the day, even if his stupidity can be amusing at times.

There's still no sign of him when Val asks, "But why would she?"

"Oh dear God. I have so much to teach you," I just barely pay attention to Lea's mutters of what sounds to be exhaustion. They've obviously spent a great deal of time together today. "He's her lover. Obviously she's concerned about where he is."

Lea chuckles slightly at his joke. Both of them have me slightly pissed off at this point and when I turn around to look at them, with the meanest scowl that I can muster for the time being, I find Val with a look of utter confusion clouding his face. Ever so slightly I hook my index finger under the edge of his plate and flip it onto his lap so that he is now wearing his food. Lea's scowl changes to match my own and only then does Val's look of confusion leave his face and he finally laughs.

I'm still looking around for Christopher when a young boy, a slave, comes in. It's very rare to see a male slave around here, especially one so young, often times the girls don't last long due to the men raping them but I've never found appeal in such a thing. There's a noticeable loss of baby fat around his face and for some reason this makes me slightly remorseful. I'm so focused on watching this ten-year-old boy that I completely forget about my search for Chris, my eyes follow the boy all the way up to the stage.

He stands there at the front of the room, looking small and timid. The boy just barely puts his lips to the mic, "Commandment has an announcement."

In the next second it's like everyone stands up at the same time and starts to make their way to the front of the room. Every Swajen elbows past those younger than them until all of the soon to graduate hug the bottom foot of the steps. As soon as Commandment enters the room, every soldier snaps into a salute so ridged that the sound of several cracking elbows is audible.

"Attention all Oslian Soldiers," The commandment of Swajen says in a voice that could burst ear drums, as if he didn't already have our attention. "There is now a new training element being added for the strongest and brightest graduating Swajens to compete in."

Several murmurs whisper throughout the room, wondering voices course through several of the younger soldiers, but for those of us above Asyme, it's very obvious who will be competing. Our highest ranking includes: Leathern (Lea), Bryan, Christopher, and finally me. This training element has to be none other than Sloeq Plan, just as Christopher was telling me except he's not even here.

"Soldier Jeffery Leathern, come forward," Commandment's voice booms and Lea walks forward, wiping his sweaty palms off on his pant legs, falling to take a knee in front of our superiors. "The Empire of Sleisia has had its eye on you since you were a young Kuswax; do you now swear unwavering loyalty to your empire and do everything commanded of you, without question?"

The whole room watches as his shaking breath announces, "I swear."

A dagger is slid out of his belt and he holds the shaking blade with his right hand. He presses the cool, sharp metal into his palm in order to swear his blood and everything he is to Oslia. Several drops are squeezed out and hit the marble in several splats at Commandments' feet. Lea gets to his feet and falls back into line with the rest of us, cradling his hand.

"Soldier Bryan Morrison, step forward," Is called out into the mass. Bryan takes the few necessary steps very confidently and immediately falls down to his knees on the steps. "The Empire of Sleisia has had its eye on you since you were a young Kuswax; do you now swear unwavering loyalty to your empire and do everything commanded of you, without question?"

"I swear!" He shouts so confidently that the noise vibrates my ear drums.

When he slits his palm open he squeezes a vast amount of blood onto the floor, several crimson puddles lay there on the floor.

"Yeah!" He screams as he gets back up to his feet.

"Soldier Valenzuar Keilly, come forward," Commandment calls out into the crowd of soldiers. Val steps forward shakely, the whole room sharing the same amount of confusion. He falls down to his knees on the steps, just as Bryan and Lea did before him.

"The Empire of Sleisia has had its eye on you since you were a young Kuswax. Will you, Valenzuar Keilly, swear unwavering loyalty to the empire and do everything that is commanded of you?"

Confusion vibrates through out the crowd as Val takes his oath, "Where's Christopher?" Someone from behind me hisses into my ear. "He should be up there; not Val."

All I can do is stay silent and listen to the rest of Val's oath because he's right, it should be Christopher up there not Val and it would be a terrible thing to take away from my friends joy. Commandments speech is now over and Val is sliding his dagger from his belt; I can't help but notice that he never actually swore. He slashes into his palm, shakely, making a shallow cut that barely allows any blood to fall to the floor. Once he's back in formation with us I can't help but look around and wonder if anyone else noticed that he never swore his oath but still drew blood.

"Soldier Kiera Pole, come forward," I am commanded. I take the few necessary steps and then fall to my knees at the feet on my superiors, my knife already gripped in my hand. "The Empire of Sleisia has had its eye on you since you were a young Kuswax; do you now swear unwavering loyalty to your empire and do everything commanded of you, without question?"

As soon as he's done talking I know it's my turn, "I swear!" I shout with an unwavering furiosity.

When I put the blade to my palm, however, I stop short. A total and complete feeling of not belonging in this life washes over me until I fear I might drown out of having no control of self belonging. Maybe this isnt my life, maybe this isn't where I'm supposed to be but I cut myself anyways and watch the puddle grow in increasing size. I stand up sharply so that people can not see the battle raging on inside me, falling back into rank with my fellow soldiers, letting the blood from my injured hand continue to hit the floor.

"These four that stand before you today will face either great reward or punishment," Head of Commandment yells out into a crowd that can only be described as feeling of growing in size at this moment. My hand reflexively balls up into a fist but the blood continues to flow hot and sticky down the side of my left hand. "They face leading Sloep Plan and dealing with the many prisoners that reside there."

Many of the younger soldiers murmur at the back of the room. It is well known that many of the world's most dangerous criminal sit rotting in there but the power that comes with being Commander over the highest ranking prison is well worth it.

"After two months service there, the four soldiers will be whittled down to two and the winners will hold high positions of power within our military and government. As price for the victor who takes second behind our champion, will become Commander over Sloep Plan."

As good soldiers, the room stays silent but the room buzzes with the electricity of what an honor it would be to run such an astemed compound.

"Then as a price only worthy of our champion, the position of second in Command to our next Emperor will be appointed."

The room stays silent as each and everyone takes in the gravity of what either of those positions could mean. As Commander over Sloeq Plan, you are one of the highest ranking soldiers in Oslian Military but to be second in command to the Emperor, you'd be practically royalty. Despite having a position, both just as grand, I can't be the only one who noticed that Commandment did not state what would happen to the two Victors who loose. For now I choose to keep that little secret to myself from my competitors, them not needing the extra incentive to cut this prize away from me. Within minutes we are dismissed and I grab both Lea and Val by the wrists, dragging them after me so that they can help me find Christopher.

We wind our way through the mess hall and out the doors that a throng of people are trying to push out of all at once. The moment that we step out onto the section of grounds that Soldiers are allowed to train on, we all spot Chris. Grasped in both of his lean hands is a shining, silver sword that is being abused into submission against a wooden post. The four of us stalk up to him and I can't help but watch with pity in my eyes as my best friend destroys that beam.

"Christopher?" I can barely bring myself to ask.

He whirls around, swinging the long, sharp sword in an arch, each of us dropping to a crouch to avoid a beheading. As soon as he sees its us, his eyes meet mine and he drops the sword in shame, sinking to a defeated posture. It's very clear that this recent set back has defeated him and for a moment I feel great shame for my friend. All I can do for him is stand silently until he picks himself back up again.

"What happened?" I ask when he's reached a soldier worthy height again.

He sucks in a breath, almost trying to absorb any of the mist that hangs in the nights grey evening, before he says, "I was approached by Commandment this morning and they said that I shouldn't have known about the new training event ahead of time," his voice is very monotone, as if he was back in time, reliving the event. "That I don't deserve the honor of Sloeq Plan; then they demoted me. But not before they gave me a citation."

That's when he truly loses it, hacking away at the ground with the sword. Quickly I Form my body to his so that way his hunched spine is pressed into my stomach, I try as hard as my short arms will reach, to pin his arms behind him. Nostalgia chokes me for a second, the feeling of him reminds me of someone else but I don't have time to dwell on it because Lea is grabbing the weapon off of the grass. Val comes over to grab underneath his right arm to help me drag him back to his dwelling. Between the three of us we manage to get him into his bunk in the barracks as visions of tucking a small boy into bed, flashes through my mind.

Just before we leave Val asks Chris a question I was hoping he never would. "Christopher. What happens to the two Victors who don't make ranking?"

Almost sleepily he replies, "They'll be banished." We all leave after that.

Chapter Four

The portal ride is long and boring without Christopher here beside me. I can't help but think about how cheated he must feel right now. There is no way that I should have made it here without him. For years we have gone back and forth between the two of us being the top of our class. If I'm going to Sloeq Plan, he should be going with me. I may be at the top of our class at this very moment but he was a very close second. Bryans score may be high but it was never as high as Christopher's. So in reality, Bryan should have barely made it in by the skin of his teeth; Lea, even that knucklehead, out ranked Bryan. The portal ride isn't as long as I initially thought it would be, what with Val and Lea jabbering in my ears the whole time.

As soon as the craft touches down we are all shown to the quarters that will be staying in for the next few weeks. It's definitely much nicer than my old room back at the Oslian's training center but not nearly as nice as my place in Oswana. There's a reasonably comfy bed that sits in the center of the room and a nice solid dresser that I hang my uniforms and plain clothes in. On the far right wall of the room there are two oak doors, one that leads to an ornate crystal bathroom. The other door leads to an extravagant office, much nicer than my one back home, a grande mahogany desk sits decorating the room.

I leave my possessions on my bed to later be put away by a maid and exit my room through the door that leads to my office. I run my fingers over the soft leather that wraps around my desk chair and push my palm down on the plush cushions of the day seater that I wish I could curl up on right now. Even the polished, golden door knob feels cool and silky against my rough skin as I leave and make my way out into the hallway. The hallways are short and efficient in this building that was built just for our Victors. Out in the middle of the sand blown desert,

Sloeq Plan sits with barbed wire fences and electrified guard gates. The doors to the prison are flung open when the guards see it's me and I am greeted with deep bows. It's strange to see men much older then me fold in half as if I am a superior to them; it's obvious on some of their faces that they aren't to fond of the idea either. Slaves rush over to me to clean the sand from my hair and clothing, dusting the sand out of my long plaited braids and freshly pressed uniform.

Once I am deemed clean of any dirt I am allowed to pass through and make my way down the dark, dank hallways. I am shown to the meeting room where my fellow Victors stand at the head of the room. Every soldier that is not currently on duty is here in this room, every last one of them saluting to me and making a path for me to get through. My days of having to elbow my way through my brutish fellow soldiers is over. Right away they start to fill us in on everything we have to know about Sloeq Plan and in no time we have the hang of the rotation schedules.

On the portal ride here we all tried to decide how it would work best to run the prison (all except Bryan). We eventually came up with a system that would give us all optimal time running the prison; all Bryan did was insist that he should be in charge full time, that or all the different ways he plans on beating us.

I step forward, my hands slightly shaky, trying to slow my breathing. "We decided that for these first two days, we will all share the responsibilities of being Commander and then switching off till we each take turns for a day," I pause to briefly look around, trying to find a confused face. "We'll start off with Victor Keilly and ending with myself."

I slink back into line, glad that my part of the explanation is over and done with. Now I can just hide in the shadow of Lea when he steps forward to speak.

"While we take turns being Commander, the rest of us will each be in charge of different sections of the compound," He says in a calm, cool voice that radiates confidence. Nothing along the lines of what I was like up there. "That way each of us will always be in charge of something; rotating the schedule throughout the time we are here so that we all get a feel for how things are run."

Finally Val speaks and I know that this meeting will soon be over. "If you would all now go back to your regular schedules. We will advise you if any changes are made."

The room slowly starts to empty and the room steadily becomes increasingly larger as all but three of the soldiers leave us.

"We've been instructed to show you around," The scraggly one out of the three speaks rather groughly.

Lea, Val, and Bryan trample down the stairs in order to fall behind two of the soldiers. The last man waits for me at the bottom of the steps and reaches his bent elbow out for me to take. I practically stomp down the stairs in disgust and slug this soldier who is far below me, in the face. He staggers back several steps, shock more than pain registered on his face, before he regains his composure and folds in half before me. I stalk right past him, my emotions raging as a boiling fire deep inside me; soon we form a small parade and march out to the halls.

Almost the whole damn thing is made up of concrete. Grey here. Grey there. Nothing but rough cement cakes these sullen walls. The whole place smells musty and a constant chill hangs in the air. It takes us a long while to get through all of the meeting rooms, it must be a solid half hour before we even reach the elevators. The seven of us squeeze into one of those small cubes, riding up floor after floor, viewing cell after cell. Every floor is designated for a specific crime; the higher up you get, the worse the crime. The main floor is mainly infectives, petty crimes, often times the crime is stealing from a soldier. A solid two floors are set aside for war criminals and people who have betrayed their country. Those cells are located just below the floor that is set aside for various interrogation rooms and cells set aside for torture. But the highest level is set aside for the mentally unstable.

"Every once and a while a prisoner is dragged up to the wacko chambers just to scare them for a night or two, to teach them good behavior," One of the soldiers, Carcossa, says as we ride up the elevator, but the soldier I punched still has yet to speak.

The doors to the elevator open and we get the faint sound of screams echoing out through the metal doors. Just before we enter, we are handed clean, white masks so that way the cotten can damper some of the smell. The whole place smells terrible, stale urine and feces pollute the air. Murmurs of begs and pleads are audible as we pass; more than once, a hand has to be kicked so their infested hands don't dirty our clean uniforms. You can almost feel the craziness in the air and in the distance an incomprehensible voice can be heard.

A little girl sits, clinging to the bars of her cell, singing something to a dead mouse in the corner. Val stays there, staring at the young girl, for several long moments. There's several small children up here. The sight is very puzzling to me; Val hardly ever cares about trivaless things such as this. Lea has to take a hold of Val just so he'll start to move even when he does, its at a very somber pace. Further down the line of cells, a man sits the chewing on his fingers and for a second I swear that I see bone. Lea almost hurls against the wall at the sight and that's when we finally leave.

We eventually ride the elevator down past all of the floors that we previously took tours of and down to what is known as the experimental levels. The elevator goes down to the first floor and we are forced to climb down the iron staircase where an elderly man waits for us. Our tour guides explain that they don't have clearance down here and they leave us with a man named Doctor Moscuwats. He's bright and bubbly; not at all my type of person. Someone comes and cleans us of any dirt or germs that we may have been carrying with us from the rest of the prison. The Doctor finally unlocks the padlocked door in front of us when the attendants leave.

We come to a clean, white room and I don't know if I should be amazed or horrified by it. Along the walls hang bodies that have a variety of tubings and wiring protruding out of their skin. Several weird contraptions litter the floor, making a maze for us to get through. Looking around the room I notice that what the Doctor is accomplishing here is really quite remarkable. He's testing a variety of different serums out on these meaningless people. Curing many dangers that could kill off our soldiers.

"This man," The Doctor surries away to point out a man with fiery blisters infecting his body. "Is our only subject to come so close to helping us concure burns instantly," The Doctor bounces excitedly, possibly thinking about the future outcomes. It's truly too bad that he'll die from all the pain soon. We've made so much progress; luckily, we have plenty of fresh subjects downstairs."

The doctor soon leads us out of his toy room and down another flight of stairs. There's another vast door at the top and bottom of the staircase, both of which require different sets of passwords. We exit out into a vast hallway, with maybe ten cells lined up on the right hand side, leading to a big metal door that doesn't even have a crack for the means of peaking in. I try to walk as tall as I possibly can, these prisoners need to sense that they are in the presence of those far superior than those they have been exposed to already. The Doctor jabbers on as we walk and several of the prisoners step forward to get a glimpse of the owners of the new voices they're hearing.

"Kieranna?" A shocked strangled voice cries from behind me.

My hand reflexively flies to the handle of one of my knives before I turn around to face the voice. In a shadowy corner of a cell, the outline of a man can barely be seen cowering in the back of the cell. I step slowly in the direction of the cell, with one of my knives out, while the Doctor and everyone else watches. The closer I get to the cell, the closer the man gets to me. I am within inches of the cell when the man jumps forward until his face is practically pushed up against the bars.

"Christopher?" I can't help but gasp in shock at seeing this familiar face behind bars.

What once was a face full of shock and joy is now a mask filled with sorrow.

"No Kier," He says sadly, reaching one hand out to try and caress my cheek.

That's when I finally notice the difference between Christopher and this man. While this man is obviously much more dirty than I've ever seen Christopher; he is far more older. A thin scar runs across his forehead and the tattoo of an Oslian soldier runs along the back of his neck but jagged skin cuts across it, the sign of several citations.

The instant his grimy fingers touch my cheek, the blade in my left hand flies through the air in an arch, slashing through flesh. The hand that was once touching my skin falls away as shouts of pain echo in the dungeon. The man falls backwards, grasping his bleeding forearm.

"That's enough Jason. Leave our poor Victor alone," Doctor Moscuwatts says with a hearty chuckle.

"Victor?" The man, Jason, asks in horror, as if it was some terrible thing.

"Yes. Victor," Lea steps forward to face the prisoner. "And you should do well to remember that because if you ever lay a finger on her again, I will personally drag you upstairs to the torture chambers."

With those words, Lea grabs me by the shoulders and places me firmly between him and Val as we continue as we continue to walk on towards the giant metal door. Jason, the man who looks so much like Christopher, watches us leave from behind, back in his cell. Something about his touch pulls at strings in my memory. You would think that years of imprisonment would hard up his hands but his skin was as soft as silk.

"How long has that prisoner been here?" I question the Doctor as we get closer to the door.

"About seven months," he replies rather cooly before turning around to face us. "This might not be fit for a lady."

All four of them eye me before Bryan says, "Very well. Pole, you stay here."

As soon as he's done speaking, Bryan follows after the Doctor. I only get a sad look from Lea and Val before they go with them. The metal door shuts with a deafening clunk and I am left out in the hall of cells by myself. Both of my knifes stay out in my hands, even if they are stuck behind bars I don't want to take any chances.

"Kiera?" Jason calls down from the end of the hallway where he lays in his cell, my name sounds like it feels foreign to him.

I inch slowly back down the hallway, weary of the man. "How do you know my name?" His dirty face looks at me from where he lays, cradling his arm. "I don't know you; we've never seen each other in my life."

He laughs from where he's at on his cot. "Oh!" There's so much sarcasm syruped in his voice that it infuriates me. "Boy do they have you trapped. They may have you believing you don't know me, but trust me Miss Pole. We know each other quite well."

Something inside me chokes and all I can say is, "You will address me as Victor Pole and nothing else."

Jason shakes his head sadly before murmuring, "This isn't you." The prisoner doesn't give me much time to think before his head pops back up again. "How's my brother? Christopher."

I slowly start to lower my arms, not quite as defensive as before. There's a strange vulnerability about him right now that makes my heart sink. Normally I'm sharp as a tack but right now I can't place him and even thinking his name makes my thought process fuzzy.

"He no longer concerns you," I snap in his face as I try to mask all the strange emotions that are coursing through me. "You should just be glad that I have the decency to spare my friend the humiliation of having a prisoner for a brother. He shall never know about this; Christopher doesn't need to lose you twice."

As soon as I finish the last syllable of my sentence, I spit at his feet, missing his right big toe by centimeters. Jason's jaw slackens just barely, as if this treatment truly shocks him.

"What did they do to you?"

His sad puppy dog eyes disgust me and I creep closer to the bars so that I can have a better look at him. Now it's very clear to me, the difference between him and his brother. Chris has green eyes while Jason has blue with grey hugging his irises. I spot scars creeping up the back of his collar from what appears to be long ago lashes and I feel a sudden pang of pride.

All of these strange, never felt before, emotions course through me and all I can say is, "You. Don't. Know. Me."

Chapter Five

That night I dream of Jason and in not a way that would be expected. In the dream we stand out in lushes trees, far past any deserts. Oddly enough birds sing even as I'm trying to hold up a large sword that he handed me. Everything about it feels real. I feel like I can actually feel the cool metal. It feels so real and familiar; it feels more like a memory than a dream. It's almost as if this occurred years previous and now I'm trapped inside my body, watching it play out. Helpless. Towards the end of the dream I awake with a start, just as soon as his arms start to encircle me. His breath tickles my ear as he starts to tell me something.

I sit up straight in bed, sweat covering my body and the sheets twisted around my ankles like a noose meant to strangle my feet. As quickly as I can, I dart to the bathroom and try to drown away the dream. Eventually I have to step out of the shower and towel off. A few maids come and twist my hair erratically into a bun at the base of my skull. They bring me a fresh uniform: a pair of tight black pants and a loose, white cotton blouse before helping me tie up a pair of knee high boots. Finally, I am brought my coat that sinches around my hips and hugs up to my collar bone before cutting off.

I dismiss them as soon as I deem my appearance worthy; as I stare at my appearance, I can't help but notice that I look far healthier than every single person stuck in those cells.

Before I head downstairs for breakfast, I stop in my office to quickly go over my schedule. I've barely even glanced at it before I spot a clean, white envelope laying there. I use one of my nails like a letter filer and open the envelope to find Christopher's handwriting scrawled at the top of the page addressed to a name I only just heard yesterday.

Dearest Kieranna,
I write this letter to you before my confidence shatters and I'll no longer be able to write. It all seems quite ridiculous, everything that has happened. Never in my life did I imagine I would get a citation. I always thought that if one of us would, it'd be you. You have always been, by far, the more rebellious one out of the two of us. Although, something like that is far beyond my worries at this moment. Right now the

whole country loves you and every soldier here at home is placing bets on who will win. Listen, I've placed a very sizable wadger on you, so you better win. But right now, in what is a very gloomy part of my life, I am very glad for you, my dear friend. To be able to witness what I can only guess is the beginning of your prime. Right now you are by far the favorite of the soldiers and I even hear from time to time that the men can't wait for the Victors Notices to be printed. Although, I imagine that the pictures haven't even been taken yet. By the time my letter reaches you, it may still be a couple days. All that I can do now is hope that you win; not just for your sake but for my own. Even now I don't want you to lose; I want to see you back home. Losing would mean that you will be banished to the desert and I have so many things I want to tell you.

It's hard to even begin to tell you over a letter. It seems truly inappropriate to tell a fellow soldier that you have feelings for them but then again it would be a lie if I told you anything different. For the last six months I have held you up high on a pedestal, Miss Kieranna. You hold a spell over me, heart and soul and nothing is going to stop that now. I truly wish that I had never even begun to feel such things. We both know you hold feelings for someone or more like something else. Rules have never been made about one soldier falling for another but then again you are the first women in history to join our country's military so there's never been much need to. A fact that you already know. Now I feel it's only right to tell you that instead of you finding out from my brother Jason.

As you well know, my brother has tried to reach out to me for the past few years and only when you left did I finally need to feel the comfort of his words. I'm sure that you know this by now but he's being kept prisoner at Sloeq Plan, underneath the experimental wards. He last wrote to me a month ago, begging me to find his long lost bride; confirming all the rumors that have been circling around. Now I write to him to regrettably inform him that she is dead. That no one will ever hear from, what he called, his dearest one again. I trust that you don't mind that I enclosed his letter with yours, I was just hoping that you could send it along to him with a slave. True, that when the letters first started coming I, regrettably, replied to him but he was always one of the best liars I know. That may be what has made him one of the best and worst soldiers we've ever had. Same could be said about you. I trust that whatever crap he tells you, you don't believe. He may be family but he is still a prisoner, one that cannot be trusted. Regrettably, in a moment of insanity, I wrote to my brother explaining my feelings to you in a plea of understanding. Now all I can do is hope that Jason listens to his brother and spare me my sanity.

As of now, I hope that you don't hate me, my dear Kiera. If you have any affections for me all you have to do is say so but if you don't, I will never mention this again. I know that this letter may have frightened you; making you wonder how awkward it will be to speak to me again. Forget about this, if you must, I just thought that it was better for me to share my affections for you just once rather than hiding them for the rest of my life. All I want now is your happiness.
All of my love for you Kieranna,
Christopher.

I lean back in my chair and hold the now crumpled letter in my hand, completely shocked. In all the time that I've known Christopher he has never once hinted at his feelings for me. Now he's pleading with me to love him the same or to never talk to him about this. What I once considered a constant in my life now lays in shambles. How can I deal with something like this when I've never had reason to give it any thought before? He now just expects me to do him a favor after he turns my world upside down. To deliver a letter to his brother because he was dumb enough not to make it here himself. Very slowly, my anger with Christopher over the arrogance of this letter builds up. I have to hold back quite a few screams before folding the crumpled letter and setting it down, just before placing the one to his brother in my pocket. I soon hastily exit my office, hoping to leave my thoughts of that letter behind.

As I trample down the hallway I can't help but roll my eyes at this nonsense. That letter could not have come at a worse time, half of the damn thing didn't even make sense. Kieranna, a name I've never heard in my life, a name that he called me three times. Now he wants me to cater to his wishes and deal with his brother who could very easily ruin everything I've been building my career to be. I can't help but practically stomp down to the dining room where everyone already waits. Sadly, everyone is seated and is able to watch me as I quickly take my seat. Lucky enough, as soon as plates of food are set in front of us, the boys forget about me. It's as if I'm eating by myself. They leave me alone with my terrible thoughts and it's a blessing when they finish. Only just now realizing that I'm still here, Lea comes and pulls out my chair and Val grabs my hand to pull me to my feet. The four of us march our way back through the sand whipped desert and ushered into the prison. Once again people come to clean us of any dirt. The only reason they get done before me is because they don't have a crap ton of hair that has to be picked through. Not short enough after we are all brought to a meeting room where we are brought new copies of our schedules. I am finally able to look at it, Christopher's letter no longer here to distract me.

I sit in that same room for hours of the day, just the four of us. Vast amounts of paperwork, forms to be signed about prisoner movement, schedules to be made. It isn't until the end of the day that I notice Doctor Moscuwatts has requested a meeting with me, the paper being so far buried under my things. I summon a slave to bring a slip of paper saying that I'll be down at the end of the day before resuming my work. Oddly enough, as we discuss what to do about execution day this Friday, Val is oddly out of it.

"Don't you worry about this Kiera. Let us men take care of this," Bryan smiles at me, pissing me off.

I can't help but grumble as Lea and I walk away to go offer the soon to be executed prisoners, their last meal. Most people think that Oswana is not gracious enough to offer such a luxury but even our enemies deserve a full stomach before walking to the gallows. Now Leathern and I must go listen to prisoners say they want to see their families one last time instead, a wish that we cannot grant. The second to last prisoner that we go to visit is up in the psych ward and as soon as we enter I press my mask as tightly as I possibly can to my face. The little girl that we saw yesterday, the one that was singing to a dead mouse, is now pulling out clumps of her hair and braiding it in her grimy hands.

I crouch down, not wanting my pants to touch the gross floor and try to whisper to her as sweetly as I can manage. "Is there any last wish you may have?"

The child's big brown eyes look up at me and I notice that there is a chunk missing out of her right ear.

"Bath," the girl mumbles before continuing to pull out clumps of hair from her scalp so she can continue her braid.

I nod at Lea slightly and we both return our masks to the guard outside the door when we leave before we ride the elevator down. Down and down we go until we make it to the Doctor's experimental wards. I give Lea a quizzical look before he nods confirming my suspicions that we are down here for a prisoner. My immediate thoughts go to Jason. For some reason it almost pains my heart for me to think it's him.

I expect the nauseatingly chirpy man to show up and lead us through to the cells downstairs but he doesn't. Lea heads over to the door on the far side of the room as the experiments call out for our help. He enters a series of numbers into the panel beside the door that leads to the "special cells". My anger flares up slightly at the thought of all the other Victors potentially having the passcodes and not me. The two of us make our way down the stairs, me stomping more than anything else, before we swing the door open to the long hallway of cells. My heart squeezes rather painfully in my chest at the thought of the prisoner we're here to see being Jason. I gladly dismiss the weird feeling when Lea stops a few cells before his.

"Mr. Bradley?" Lea asks the man that sits before us behind the cell's bars. The man sits up and nods at us as Lea puts his list of prisoner names away into one of his many jacket pockets. "As you have been informed, your execution date is this Friday. Do you have any requests?"

The man, Mr. Bradley, jumps into civilized conversation with Lea about how he would like a good steak and potato again. My mind soon wanders as the two discuss arrangements for his final request and I start to wonder what Jason is doing.

"Kieranna?" A timid voice calls to me from a couple cells down.

I sneak a glance down at Lea before I slink along the wall and towards Jason's cell. He's laying down on the hard concrete floor just staring at the ceiling until he sees me then he immediately jumps to his feet. Jason now stands, pressing his body up against the bars so incredibly hard, he stares at me with such intensity that I must look away for just a moment.

"What's with that name?" I ask, my heart clenching because it doesn't belong to me.

"Are you the one sentencing people?" He follows up my question with one of his own, testing my patience the same way his brother does.

With my patience now lax, I reach into my pocket and pull out the letter from Christopher. My hand shakes slightly as I pass it to him through the bars. The faint brush of his skin against mine causes tingles to go through not just my fingers but my entire arm.

"This letter came for you today; its from your brother," I breath as he opens the envelope and starts to read.

The longer it takes him to read, the more awkward I start to feel. I glance over at Lea to make sure that he is still occupied with the other prisoner. It takes Jason a good few minutes to read the letter and by the time he's done, he has tears in his eyes. My disgust for him grows a bit, seeing that he's so mushy.

"Have you read this?" His sadness quickly changing to anger.

I quietly shake my head, unnerved by his drastic change of mood. This kind of emotion does not look well on his features.

Jason then proceeds to read the letter aloud to me…

My brother Jason,
As I'm sure you can imagine, it is a huge burden on the family to have the disgrace that is to have you as a relative. It has been a struggle to now build up a once pristine reputation, one that you tarnished with your first citation.

He pauses briefly and I can't help but admire what a sweet reading voice he has. That is until a deep pang fills my chest because Christopher is lecturing him about something he himself did.

You gave everything up for a girl who can no longer remember you. You've given up a comfortable life for nothing. By now assume you've seen Kieranna and you must know that everything I've written is true. The only way that she knows you now is as my disgruntled, disgrace of an older brother. Sure, this now sounds like such a tragic love story since you wrote to me to find your 'dearest one'. It's true that I did find her but not in the sense that you may have liked. Somehow I have fallen deeply in love with this girl. I know that the old you would have lectured me about having such affections for a fellow soldier but you are in no position now. As of now I feel like it is truly inappropriate for me to plead with you but I feel like I must. If you spare Kieranna, I may be able to negotiate a pardon for you that could get you out of jail. It cannot possibly be worth being imprisoned for one girl.

Jason pauses to look up at me and I can't place the emotion there but there is a deep warmth behind his eyes.

I'm sure that even you have noticed that Kiera made it to Sloeq Plan while I have not. That is purely because her abilities have far surpassed even mine or yours. Why try and ruin the life that she built up, with history? When you last wrote me, you said you wanted to be able to see your dear Kieranna happy again. Well, now she is and I know that you would never want to obscure that by bringing back all of the haunting memories that her former life held. Write to me when you come to a decision and I'll negotiate a pardon. You know what the right decision is.
                              Your brother.

The both of us stay silent for a long time after he's finished reading. He stares at me, just waiting on me to say something but I don't know how. Nothing that was read makes any sense; the way Christopher wrote about me makes it sound like I've lived this whole other life with entirely different people and memories. The way that Christopher mentioned to me, the letter he wrote to his brother sounded nothing like what he said it would be. It's almost laughable in a way that is almost ridiculous.

Christopher chatisized his brother for getting so many demerits but that's what he did just a few days ago. He is in no position to be negotiating any sort of pardon for any person. That dumbass sure made certain that letter couldn't be traced back to him by not even signing his name. The only way someone could find out that it was from him is because he enclosed Jason's letter with mine but he never mentioned that to Jason.

Very slowly, I am able to focus my attention back on Jason and look him in the eyes despite my endless string of waiting questions.

"That girl in the letter…" I stutter. "You think she's me?"

"No," he says, looking at me with unwavering certainty. "I know that you're her."

Normally, I would never be intimidated by someone as lowly as Jason, let alone anybody, but his stare is so intense that I must look away.

"Your brother won't be able to pardon you," I say, not wanting him to get his hopes up. "I'll be back later for you to answer my questions."

With the very last bit of my sanity, I scamper off towards Lea, leaving Jason far behind.

Chapter Six

The meeting room back at our quarters is a complete buzz tonight and I can't help but rub my temples as I try to fend off a headache that is sure to come from the commotion.

"No! No! No!" Bryan shouts at the rest of us. "We have to start the power transitions before we get our review this Friday. We have to be 100% comfortable with these transitions before Commandment gets here."

Right away Val and Lea start to argue with Bryan about this not being in our original plans. The screaming eventually becomes too much and I interject.

"I agree with Bryan," I speak up for the first time in a solid hour.

Those four words now invite two of my best friends to direct their yelling at me. I kind of grumble in pain back at the two of them while they screech at me.

"Well done, mi amor," Bryan slurs with satisfaction, speaking in the same tongue the slaves use.

My stomach squeezes in disgust at the phrase Bryan called me. I want to take back my statement purely out of my hate for him but I must at least put up the facade that I have a backbone. The two of them exhaust the topic until we have all drank a combined bottle of whiskey and my head is officially pounding. All four of us sit collapsed in different chairs about the room. My mind fuzzes in and out of focus so much that I can barely focus on the screen in front of me. I think it holds part of a schedule for tomorrow but I can't be sure because all I want to do is escape to my room and call on a slave to bring me a glass of water.

"That's enough!" I finally stand up from my chair and scream. "Our plan starts tomorrow with Lea in charge."

Lea perks up considerably just before Val and Bryan stock off towards the door, both of the big brutes fighting to get out first.

I head over to the door, hoping to shut it as soon as they both leave but Bryan calls to me while he's walking down the hallway.

"You really command a room, Fiera," My eyebrows furrowed together at being called 'the fire one' by Bryan, he never has before. "But you could have done better."

The name is soon forgotten when I roll my eyes because better in his terms could only mean him. I practically slam the door behind him and I hurry back over to Lea. Leathern now sits at the table examining a lay out of the schedule, trying to figure out how to place everyone.

"May I see that?" I hold out my hand tentatively, asking for the schedule.

He passses it over to me and I pretend to look like I'm struggling to place everyone. I write down Val's name down first, placing him in charge of the interrogation floors, and I then place myself working downstairs with the Doctor. Once I get the spot I want all I have to do is place Bryan. The only place I can think of that is terrible enough to match his personality would be the psych wards so I write his name down there before passing the pages back to Lea with an evil grin splitting across my face. Both of surprisingly get to leave this meeting with a smile on our faces.

That night it takes me forever to fall asleep. Even when I do sleep it's very fitful; I toss and turn, frightened by the film that plays its way through my head. Nothing is concrete and I only get snippets of things before they change. At first I'm running for what feels like decades, with a rather handsome man. My feelings are a strange mix of shock and betrayal but the scene soon changes when a pair of strong arms catch me around the middle. Now I'm younger and walking hand in hand with a boy around the age of four. From the vague sights I see, I can tell that we are walking through an Infective market place. The feeling of an item in my hand draws my gaze to the left but when I look down all I can see is the dirt caking my skin. It looks like I haven't had a bath in weeks, that's when the landscape is altered again.

I stand in a house with cracked paint and a ceiling that is barely holding itself together looms over me, but I think that I am the happiest I've ever been. I am very young now, only a year younger than the boy, several different women whirl around me in a kitchen that is almost ancient. They sing and speak in a language that I can't quite understand but I know that they are overjoyed to be this busy. I stand there smiling at everyone's thighs until someone picks me up and sits me down at a table with dough on it for me to play with. All the women soon start to sing in that same language as they continue to cook. I want to join in on the merriment but I don't know the words even though I know I've heard the song a half dozen times before. My mind becomes puzzled and my body starts to shake, the images snap.

"Ma'am?" A slave asks, shaking me until I'm awake.

I instantly freeze up at the thought of a slave touching me and my arm flies up to back hand her across the face. The woman's touch falls away when she realizes her wrong doing, only then am I able go throw the covers off of my body. On my way to the bathroom I shudder, remembering the feeling of the slaves hands on me. In the powder room several more slaves wait to help me into the tub that is full of water and lavender oils. The amount of time that I sit soaking in the tub is not nearly long enough. My attendants jabber around me and from what little I understand from their words, I slept in far too late.

I am soon rushed out of the tub, even though I could have soaked for several more hours, then numerous hands descend upon me to help me towel off. Once I am dry, they plop me down in a chair and start to brush through my long curls, pinning them to the nape of my neck. They've just pinned the last strand of hair to my head when there's a soft knock on my office door. The young slave that I slapped earlier leaves us as the rest finish wiping swipes of black around my eyes. Clothes are brought to me and I slip on a pair of dark green slacks with a tight black blouse that has the Slesia flag on the sleeve. Lastly, a pair of heeled ankle boots are brought to me and they pinch my toes as I walk into my office. I open the door and Lea stands in front of my desk clutching a folder to his chest, gazing at me.

He stands there waiting for me to sit in my chair, only when I collapse into a sitting position does he take a seat across from me. Without a single word he passes me the folder that he was clutching to him minutes ago. Inside the flaps is document after document, each one requiring me to sign or initial something.

"What are these?" I ask, throwing the folder back at him.

He leans forward slightly before saying, "You put yourself down for supervising the experimental ward. The Doctor asked if you would sign these forms saying that everything you witness is legal and morally abiding by Sleisia's laws."

He once again passes the papers back to me and this time when I take them I actually take a good look at them. Going through the papers I notice that every single prisoner down there is a war criminal that we've captured and forced into experimentation. Only when a prisoner volunteers can they back out.

"What kind of shit is this?" I ask, cursing at him, wondering what type of lunacy goes on down there.

Lea tilts his head to the side in confusion before saying, "I don't understand what you mean."

"These," I say, grabbing a fistful of papers before shaking them in his face. "They can't possibly be true. There is no way anyone would volunteer to take part in that madness. I can't possibly imagine the Doctor letting anyone out of there."

I practically throw the documents back at him, suddenly feeling like nothing I've ever done is morally right. Guilt surges through me and I don't feel like myself. Never once have I ever felt guilty about anything. Something is seriously wrong with me but I can't shake this feeling. Very suddenly, Lea reaches forward across the table and grabs my chin so sharply that I am pulled out of my seat towards him. Our faces are now inches apart, this is the maddest I've ever seen him; he never relinquishes his hold on my chin.

"This is what soldiers do!" He spits in my face. "We lie, cheat, and steal for our country. We've trained for such a thing; you can't waste it now just because you refuse to sign a few papers."

It takes a lot of courage for me to answer but eventually I work my jaw enough to say, "I'm sorry, Lea; I can't do it." All of a sudden I feel very weak and scared, nothing at all like myself.

He gets up, finally letting go of me, scowling. "I'll move you to a different ward for the day." My heart drops down to my toes as this sentence shatters my plans for the day. The thought of not getting my questions answered by Jason, about that letter, today makes me change my mind about signing. "But I must ask you to never breathe a word about me letting you change wards after seeing those papers. Understood?"

"No," I say forcefully, getting up out of my chair and grabbing one of my pens. "I'll sign. It's the right thing to do," I force the words through my teeth.

Lea doesn't look at all surprised by me changing my mind and he hands the folder back to me. Surprisingly, there are even more papers for me to sign than I had originally thought. My initials, K.A.P. dot several pages worth of documents before I sign my name at the bottom of the pages, Kiera Annaleez Pole. As I sign my name for what feels like the millionth time, I start to notice the similarities between Kiera Annaleez and Kieranna. I try to push my qualms away by signing my signature on the last page's dotted lines.

The day starts out very slowly and I'm not able to get the work that I want to get done, accomplished right away. I've always thought that Lea had a way for words but today, holy shit, will he not shut up. I'm so anxious to get my to-do list accomplished that I fear I may go bang my head against a concrete wall. He said this would only take a few minutes but we've now been here a full hour. By the time he finishes I have an acute pain in my head and an odd twitch in my leg due to impatience. Just before I am able to slip out of the room, Lea hands me a thick portfolio filled to the brim with reports for me to read. It's slightly uncomfortable to carry all of these private words that previous soldiers have written; past the prying eyes of numerous prisoners. Once I'm in the elevator, my muscles start to loosen at the thought of getting my work done.

Eventually the elevator opens and hands pull me from the metal room, snatching the portfolio from me. Something chokes in my throat when the Inferior takes something vital and secret to our soldiers, from my hands. It takes almost all of my will power not to take it right back from her. Once they deem me free of any sort of element that I may have brought down from the prison, they let me pass through the clean room with my portfolio.

I now clutch the thing tightly to my chest as I make my way forward, afraid that someone may take it away from me again. As I open the door I notice that the burn victim is now gone, replaced by another man that the Doctor is studying profusely. Dr. Moscuwatts sits in front of him, taking hurried notes on a legal pad, watching as the new subject withers in his sleep.

"Ah . . . Victor Pole!" He says without turning around, just sensing that its my gaze that rests on him.

"Feel free to look around," His voice almost sounds like its bordering madness. "Although I must ask that you don't touch anything. We wouldn't want you to lose one of your pretty fingers."

I clamp my teeth so that I may not spill how sexist I found his comment which would reveal my newly developed insecurities. The file stays tight in my grasp as I move towards a subject that is strapped to a wooden board under the luminescent lights. The female subject stays there, rocking back and forth, trembling in pain; not even noticing my approach.

Trapped to the foot of the bed is a sheet written up on the experimentations that she has undergone. From what little that I understand, the Doctor has tried (unsuccessfully) to implant male specimen reproductive tissue into this woman so that she may self impregnate at will. So far it seems to be that her body is rejecting the Doctor's experiments; he's clearly detected that her body is bleeding from the inside out from her womb, killing her because her body is refusing to do as its commanded. He tries to express his sorrow for the failing experiment because the Doctor believes that this will help us rid of mental and physical disabilities with the similar DNA.

This could possible come with more then just stronger mental cells but come with a faster birthing rate that could produce soldiers faster with no worry of losing the child during birth.

My hands immediately drop the clip board; as a I feel wildly violated. The Doctor is trying to combine this woman's uterus with sperm tissue so that she'll become a baby making factory. He talks of free will so that she may self-impregnate but the Doctor makes it sound like this would be only for the purpose of producing more, better soldiers. The bile in my throat rises up a bit more when the thought that men consider women not to be their equal.

I force myself to move away from the metal slats as a steady puddle of blood grows from underneath the girl's thighs. Somehow I manage to back straight up into what appears to be half a metal coffin with a saw attached to the top. I've just picked up the rap sheet so that I may read the Doctor's notes when a thick male hand falls on my shoulder. I jump back and spin slightly halfway around so that I catch the end of Doctor Moscuwatts chuckles.

"I see that you have found our pride and joy," He says, gazing fondly at the metal contraption. "Would you like me to explain it to you?"

I give a slight nod of my head with my lips pressed tightly together so that way nothing vile falls out of my lips. "This device helps us make our soldiers more manageable or more agreeable. That is so our Commandment and dear Emperor don't have to waste their time squabbling with pesky soldiers," He laughs heartily, his thin, snake lips parted in amusement. Once he sees that I am not amused he lets his laughter die as my scowl deeps in my features. "Our brains are made up many different parts: parietal lobe, Medial Temporal Lobe, and Frontal Lobe. Each of these sections have some job, whether it be to control your vision, emotions or itelligence. What we are doing is extracting different, very favorable traits, and putting them into a host subject who already has desired traits," I look at him with confusion, not fully understanding what the machine has to do with it. "This machine goes in through the subject's ear and removes a desired portion of the brain, with something similar to tweezers. Then another subject will be trapped on the table and the process will begin again."

I nod along, starting to comprehend what it is the Doctor is trying to explain. From my understanding, they take someone whose brain does not have a great deal of desired traits but may have one or even two, in the hopes of further improving our soldiers. They strap one of our men down and extract their weakest portion of the brain, whether that be intelligence, stability, or personality. Then they take the portion of the brain removed from the first subject and insert someone else's traits that are more desirable.

"This could completely change the way that our army functions!" The Doctor continues on happily. "Every soldier would be more agreeable so there'd be no reason for us to have a citation system. It would be like every soldier would be the best of the best. It would be like every soldier is like our Victors. These changes to the brain could make it so we change entire personalities! By mixing the Cerebellum, the emotional portion of the brain, and the Medial Temporal which is the host for the Limbic System that holds all of your memories, you could change someone's whole personality. If you replaced one subjects Medial Temporal with others and then replace their Cerebellum you could make them into a whole new person!"

The Doctor appears to be practically giddy with excitement, just thinking about the possibilities. None of this makes sense to my mind; none of this should be possible. Nobody should have to go through something like this. All of a sudden I know why Lea made me sign all of those documents, everything that is going on down here is completely barbaric. There is no way that this could ever get out to the public, there would be mass hysteria amongst the people. My mind is spinning and the Doctor continues to go on about all of the wonderful benefits that a machine like this could pose.

"And we've barely begun testing but the subjects that have undergone the treatment have responded greatly," His voice booms loudly with joy, as he gives a clap of his large hands.

I force myself to laugh along with him, I place my hand on top of his that rests on my shoulder so that way I can pull it off. He slightly trembles at my touch and I have to gently push his hand off so that way he can't tell how much he disgusts me.

"If you don't mind," I say, trying to back away from him slowly. "I will just be heading downstairs to do my work."

I back towards the door that leads to the downstairs cells but when I try to open the door, it beeps loudly at me and won't budge. My anger suddenly flares because I once again realize that the others got the passwords and I didn't. I stand there nodding at the door while he stands there shifting from foot to foot.

"Do you mind?" I snap at him but he doesn't make any move to come unlock the door. "Well?"

"It's just that…" But the Doctor stops. I raise my eyebrows as my scowl once again over takes my features. "Nothing down there is fit for a woman."

A snarl forms at the back of my throat and it just barely stays there. "I am your Victor and anything that is suitable for the rest of your Victors, is suitable for me!" I shout, practically jumping down his throat.

His eyes wide in surprise and he scurries around me to punch a series of digits into the keypad so that the door swings open. I march straight past him and down the stairs. What does he think isn't suitable for me down here when he's willing to show me all of his gruesome experiments? All they are is a bunch of prisoners and they're even trapped behind bars! I march my way down the rest of the stairs and swing the door open to the sound of chatter going on among the prisoners. The mumbles die down as soon as the first of the prisoners spot me. All of them retreat further into their cells; all except one. I completely ignore him and turn around, expecting to see a chair set up for me to do my work, even when there is none. So I turn around and position myself on the floor, in a corner, grateful that the cells are on the other side of the room. I position the folder on my lap and dive in.

The whole folder is filled to the brim with reports from post soldiers that I've never heard of, that have passed through this prison. On the top page a note from Lea says that 'I am to read these so that we may find any sort of evidence that would be cause to put them into the prison.' After an hour of searching through the papers, I become restless.

Each of these reports is as impersonal as the last; every one of these is written by someone I've never heard of. It's taxing on my brain to go through what are mostly raid reports. All of these reports are written by computer, so no person can tell a change of writing time or if they were distracted by something because they could always come back to it. I pull down hard on some of the hairs that have escaped from the knot on the back of my head in frustration. None of these reports would suggest any of these men should end up being imprisoned. I fold up the portfolio rather roughly and shove myself up to my feet. Clutching the thing tightly under my armpit I take a few steps forward so that I am standing in front of Jason's cell. He lays there on his chest on the filthy floors with a pen clutched tightly in his right hand as papers litter the floor space in front of him. He doesn't look up as I inch closer to the bars so that way I can admire the elegant scroll of his handwriting.

"You people seem to enjoy keeping me entertained just as I am in the cusp of being abused, just so I won't think to strongly about escaping," Jason says without looking up from his work.

"Well it would make us look bad if we let a prisoner go," I say with a hearty chuckle that I can't remember the last time using. He looks up with amused surprise and I have to look away because his stare causes my body to feel weird emotions. "What are you doing with that?" I ask, pointing at his work.

He glances at the papers and then back at me, putting the cap on his pen. "It's a book; I enjoy writing. It must be something I picked up from writing all of those reports," I look down at the slightly browned papers in amazement. "You used to say that I always belonged amongst the Infective because they are the writers in our country."

Jason smiles down at his papers before shuffling them and putting them in a neat pile on something that could never pass for a bed. Once he's done, he stands up and moves towards the bars and that's when I finally notice how skinny he is. Months of malnutrition is clearly wasting away at his body; every bone in his face, arms, and chest are visible. I can't even begin to guess what disaster is going on with his legs.

"Who was I to you?" The question falls from my lips, one that I did not plan on asking.

"Someone very, very important," He responds with a loving gaze in his eyes.

"And your wife was …?" I start to ask before his vile tone cuts me off.

"Long taken from me."

I jump back slightly because his harsh tone frightens me a bit; I don't think I like Jason this way. I try and swallow down the lump in my throat because for some reason this deeply pains me. My hand starts to reach out on its own accord and just for a second my fingers skim his knuckles before I remember myself. His eyes track my fingers, hungrily, as they return to my side.

"Apparently," I start out. Trying to find the right way to phrase my question. "You and Christopher both seem to think that I once lived this other life. That you and I were once very important to each other?"

"Yes," He nods his head at me. "Still are."

His words earn one of my famous eye rolls, something Chris says when I'm feeling particularly sarcastic. Or at least I think it was him who started saying that but I can no longer be certain.

"Then why is it I can't remember any of it?" I question, thinking all the way back to my first days at Oslia and how each of them is filled with memories. "I can't remember seeing you walk around the grounds at Oslia when I was a young Kuswax. Surely Christopher would've pointed you out to me."

Jason's brow creases slightly before straightening out with a light hearted laugh. "No you wouldn't. And that's because you didn't grow up in Oslia," I look at him, slightly confused, just waiting to hear the rest of his lies. "You grew up in Eminia, a small town with all of your aunts and cousins. Your own mother died in childbirth," There is a bell of truth to what he says. My mother did die due to complications from childbirth but it was due to illness. We lived in the world's most expensive capital; you only die if there's nothing else left that can help you but you die comfortable.

"Then came the plague that washed throughout all of Sleisia. killing your family. I think that you even got sick briefly. Scars still line your body." I never could have gotten the plague as a child, soldiers are vaccinated at birth. "From then on you were out on the street on your own with a few surviving cousins," Jason says continuing on. "After that most of you were captured, this was when you were around the age of ten, and trafficked as slaves. For two years you worked as a maid before you managed to escape with your cousin, Sebastian. After that you two ended up living for a few years, then we met when you were sixteen."

My head is spinning with information and I forget that I have the portfolio in my hands. I let it drop as both of my palms come up to clutch at both sides of my head. There is no denying that some of his lies do make actual sense; my dream of walking down a slave town and when I dreamt about those women singing around a kitchen. Although, so much of it can't be true.

"If any of that is true," I say, lowering my hands and noticing that the folders contents are scattered all over the floor. "There is a flaw, I could never have been a slave. I can't speak their language."

Jason tilts his head to the side in confusion. "You can't?" he asks in complete shock.

I shake my head in response to this lunatic. "That is so strange," He mumbles, looking down at his hands that's clutch at his cell bars. "You're the one that taught me."

I then look down at my hands too, his stories are no longer amusing me. His story is actually starting to hurt me a bit, and his words bring me a fresh wave of strange emotions that I am not prepared to deal with. I stoop down to pick up the contents of my folder, only so that I can hide my face. By putting all of the papers back in with ease, only then am I able to stand and face him. Jason backs away when he sees the expression written on my face; clearly I'm not as good at hiding my fear as I once thought. Shame riddles through my body like guilt and I must back away to the door so that I can keep an eye on the prisoners as I leave. I've pushed down on the handle but it stays firmly in place. I have to bang hard against the door until the Doctor comes to investigate the source of the noise.

"I need those codes!" I say hautely as I shove my way past him and up the stairs.

Chapter Seven

I only have fifteen more minutes left of my break before I must return back downstairs to the Doctor. All of the papers from my folder are spread out on the table of my desk back at my quarters with a pen poised in my hand. Each of these reports are as dull as the last but I make small notes in the margins so that it at least appears that I am doing something with them. There are reports written by a Lawrence, a Charles, and a Jason Vierlac. Jason Vierlac, my heart stops beating from within my chest. With shaky fingers I pull out the report from amongst the other papers.

Entry No. 1056
Soldier Jason Vierlac
Raid Report

As follows, a Raid on the Sagewynne in the city ████████████, Slesia, a total of ten kills were spread out amongst the variety of soldiers sent on the raid. A young boy at the age of four was allowed to escape from my own stupidity. ███████████ escaped out into the street from the shop where a young girl ██████████, was waiting for him. With to many Infinitive around it made it impractical for the soldiers on duty to retrieve him. Now I face the Commandment and will take on my punishment /demerits as I deserve.

I practically fall forward on to my desk as I scramble to find the next entry, but there isn't one. Letting your kill go a raid is punishable by several demerits, until the point you're no longer a soldier and living as a Infective. This is what had to make Jason an outcast but it doesn't explain why he's in jail or why names and places are blacked out. Not in a single one of the other reports has a name or a place blacked out. I am ready to bang my head against the desk in frustration when the door to my office bangs open. Bryan stands in the doorway panting, as he ran all the way from the prison.

"You know you're not welcome in my private quarters," I snap at him as I try to shuffle all the reports back into their folder.

"Come quick," He says, gasping as he holds a stitch in his side. "There's been a breach in the psych ward."

Right away I am on my feet and running after him. The two of us run through the luxuriously carpeted halls and down the stairs only stopping at the door before the kitchens. Both of us select a variety of weapons such as knives and stuff them into various pockets as well as boots. When both of us have a weapon clutched into our hands, I stuff an extra gun into the waistband of my pants. The wind seems to sense the mood of the compound because it whipps around us furiously as soon as we step outside. Sand storms around my face to the point I can no longer see. My hand reaches out instinctively at Bryan's shoulder so that if I do get lost I won't be all by myself. His hand reaches back and clasps his hand in mine; this is the first time that I don't mind him touching me. He pulls the two of us towards the door and as soon as we enter we're both coughing up mouth fulls of sand. Several slaves rush to our sides so that they may clean the sand away from us but we both wave them off. Lea waits outside, loaded to his teeth with weaponry just like the two of us.

"Where's Val?" I ask breathlessly.

I expect Lea to turn around and tell me that he'll be coming any minute but when he doesn't Bryan turns to me instead. "He's the one that broke the prisoner out," Bryan's voice is rough like this might actually be affecting him. "That makes him a traitor."

My heart sinks down to my toes in disbelief; it's not like Val to even think about doing stuff like this. My hand strays to the handle of my gun so I can grip it before swinging it in front of me. The knife that was in my hand drops reflexively to to floor, knowing that there won't be any survivors. The other two follow my lead, but Lea does so much more reluctantly. Soldiers are dispersed to go search for Val while the prison goes on lockdown. Bangs sound throughout the concrete walls while the gates shut. We slowly break out of our pack and scatter ourselves throughout the hallways. Along the way I pick up a few soldiers that are currently searching the premises, always watching my back like Chris does. At even the slightest rustle of noise, all of us turn, expecting to see the traitor right in front of us. The only noises that accompany us are the sounds of prisoners begging to be let out.

We continue to move on despite their pleas, always on guard. By using the back doors that lead throughout the staircases we climb up and up and up. Several times we exit out onto different floors, searching, hoping to find some evidence that he's been here. After a few more flights, we exit out onto another floor that has several of it's cell doors flung open with no occupants. My nerves are frayed by now. The searching is getting to me, my mind is starting to play games. He's now let loose prisoners, finding them will take even more of our time.

"Go find them!" I snarl at three of my soldiers, and they rush to find the missing prisoners.

With the four soldiers that I have left we are about to head back and regroup, but there is a loud clatter that makes me turn my head. A man falls out of one of the cells as if he has been pushed out. Clutched in his hand is the little girl I saw the other day in the psych ward. Val spots us and makes a run to get out the door behind us.

"Stop!" I scream at him as my soldiers rush forward in an attempt to catch him.

My heart hammers in turn with my feet as they slam into the cement in an attempt to catch up. The girl must be slowing him down because Val should be able to get further ahead, not trapped in between my soldiers when I catch up. The gun that is clenched tightly in my hands flies up in front of me as my body realizes that I've just cornered my prey. Pathetically enough Val turns in circles, taking a turn pointing the gun that he holds at each of us in turn. The little girl whimpers as Val spins her around and round with him in the close quarters of the staircase. She clutches even tighter at Val's coat when I start to close in on them.

"Give it up Val," I try to say in my most authoritative voice that does not involve a snarl. "And maybe I can negotiate a pardon and not an execution for the both of you."

I try and play on his sympathy just like how it's playing on my heart strings. It takes a great deal to push down, what Christopher calls, my womanly instincts. Despite how much that phrase pisses me off, I can't let my need to protect this girl interfere with my duty.

"You of all people should know that I can't do that. But there is no way you would because you can't remember who you truly are!" Val spits at me and my body fills with this weekling type of pain that brings a sting to my eyes. "They've put this disgusting monster inside you that has eaten up anything good."

By now he's shouting at me and half of me wants to climb back inside myself and hide, but something else is telling me to fight back. That may be what makes me so forceful with him, and something that feels detached with myself takes over. I throw the young girl into the waiting arms of one of my soldiers. I can barely get the word gentle out of my mouth before I resume my attach on one of my best friends. He's now on his knees with the gun out of his hands before I can even blink my eyes twice. My memory panics and I can't tell if he voluntarily fell before me or if I forced him to. As I sputter about, one of my soldiers gets him into cuffs for me as my brain tries to reassemble itself. Eventually, hes hauled to his feet and I clutch the metal chain in my hands, with my weapon trained on him.

"Find the other Victors," I order one of my remaining soldiers just before he leaves us. I nod at my man who holds onto the little girl before ordering, "She'll go into the same cell as him."

Our procession is slow but productive as we march our way down, several prisoners are shoved back into their cells. Val's face falls more and more as he watches the people that he attempted to free be pushed back into custody. Alarms are still going off , and it's starting to cause a ringing to vibrate through my ears. They only turn off when Val and I once again join the other Victors. Bryan stands there, practically snarling, but Lea has a look of pain on his face. I'm not a hugger but in this moment I would consider giving him one.

"He'll go downstairs with the other traitors." Bryan nods along with my command, as Lea does nothing.

Val gets towed along rather roughly and as soon as we've descended the steps, the Doctor runs on ahead to get the doors open. The procession is slow with all the people, but there is a loud ruckus from the prisoners when they see one of their Victors in chains. A cell is flung open; regrettably, it is the cell next to Jason's. He gazes on from the bars as I shove Val down onto the floor. Valenzuar stays there in the dirt until the little girl is deposited in there as well, and the cell is locked.

"We'd like to have a word with the prisoner," Bryan snaps at the soldiers that remain.

Soon they leave us and it's just the three of us facing a hallway full of prisoners; I feel just as trapped as the rest of them. I wait silently, expecting Bryan to say something, anything, but he just stands there brooding. All the while Jason looks on at the scene looking from Val to me, and back again. There's a strange mixture of hurt and sorrow on his face, it obscures his features in a way I do not like.

"What do you have to say for yourself?" I question Val. My voice comes out in a choked croak. I have to clear my throat several times over.

Val lays there whimpering not saying a word, and it aggravates me. All I want to do is bang on the steel bars and force him to answer my questions, but that won't do any good. Instead I fall before him, on my knees, not knowing what I'm doing, but knowing I want answers. One of my hands reaches through the bars, hoping a gentle touch will open him up. I'm not able to reach Val, but the little girls crawls forward to place her hand in mine. My eyes widen in surprise, this is not the touch I was expecting. She sits there playing with each one of my fingers in turn as if she's playing some little game in her mind.

"I couldn't leave her,"a tiny whisper comes from Val, it's so quiet that I almost don't hear it.

"What?" Bryan snaps rather forcefully.

"No one deserves to die like that. Madeline didn't deserve to die like that!" Val is screaming by now and Lea's face falls. His sister, of course.

I gently extract my hand away from the girl and a look of utter disappointment covers her ashen features.

"That wasn't your call!" I snarl, getting back up to my feet. Each of my joints pop and crackle in protest.

Jason stares at me in shock and his expression is what does it for me. I storm down the hallway and stop short at the door, pausing to glare at the other remaining Victors. They have to come and unlock the door for me as my embarrassment flares up. My scowl feels like it is permanently etched into my skin when I stomp back up the stairs.

That night I sit at my desk, unable to sleep, writing out a report to commandment, asking if they'll spare Val and the girl. I know that my efforts are probably futile and won't do anything besides get me in trouble but I feel I must try. Eventually the report is finished and I lens back in my chair, resting before starting my ritual of getting ready for the night. There's a deep ache in the base of my scull and I must lay my head back against the cool leather where I shut my eyes.

Colors dance behind my lids and my lips pull up into a pleased smile, despite the pain. The colors all blend together and paint together a scene that is almost like a memory due to how familiar it is. It's rather grey out, as if it's raining (maybe it's snowing) but I get a sense of home from deep within my heart. A full sized bed is pushed to one side of what should be a cupboard but is actually a bedroom. A dress that looks like it was made by rough wood, by someone who wasn't sure what he was doing. The same goes for the bed that I am laying on with a rough blanket thrown over me.

Another body is pressed up against me, emanating it's warmth, all the while a soft heart beat thrums into the back of my rib cage. A man's arm is thrown over me and I snuggle back into his warmth, gazing at the pictures in the dresser. I breathe in his rich, spicy scent, a smell that I have now come accustomed to as Jason's. My body startles itself out of the pleasant vision and I feel myself slip into a pout. For some reason, something as simple such as being in that barren room made me happy for a minute.

That happiness doesn't stay though, because images once again swirl in my mind, bringing me to a time that my body does not want to experience. The image is blurry, almost faded in spots as my mind recalls waves of pain raking my body. A head splitting pain slams into my skull, much worse than it actually hurts in reality. I recall raising my hand up in front of my eyes (that's when I know I am much younger due to the evidence from my short, plump fingers) and feeling horror constrict my chest at seeing angry red sores cover my hands. My eyes pop open and I feel that same horror pulsate in my chest, yet this time it's for a different reason. This is the first time I've ever pictured something such as those images while I was awake. I can no longer trick my mind into thinking these are just dreams. My bottom lip quivers when I bring up both of my hands and see that those pale, white scars look like the long since healed pattern of those angry blisters. Both of my hands fall down into my lap as my fist closes up. All that pain is hard to ignore. When I feel it again for what seems like a second, it's excruciating. Pathetically, I crawl over to my bed as another wave of it hits me, when I end up collapsing there fully clothed.

Chapter Eight

I wake up that next morning, my head still pounding but I'm fully aware that it is execution day. My head lulls around on my shoulders as my slaves get me ready. With a few small tugs I am shoved into tight pants, boots, and a jacket that make up my dress uniform. My hair flows, uncharacteristically free down my back in soft ringlets. The odd hairstyle takes my mind back to simpler times and a bliss over takes my senses. I stop short on the stairs, pulling my fingers out of the smooth strands, disoriented by that new feeling. I force myself to move on, leaving my hair alone and and go to the dining room where I'm supposed to eat with Bryan and Lea. Inside the room, both the men wait for me plus one more. Christopher sits at the table with his back to me and for some reason, a bitter feeling rises up inside me. He turns around (just like the other two) when he hears me come in. Rather foolishly, he's out of his chair and helping me into mine, in a ridiculous fashion.

"Kiera," He breaths with such warmth, his hands brushing against my arms as he pushes my chair in.

"Soldier Vierlac," I say icily, he backs away from me and returns back to his seat as if I've hurt him.

Unnervingly enough, I always feel a bit of spite for myself whenever I see Jason hurt but when Chris appears to be, I think he's ridiculous. Christopher sits there and looks at me rather quizzically as if there's something off about me. It takes me a minute to actually realize that I may in fact be a little different from when he last saw me a few days ago. I may not know what is going on with me right now but I do know that it's not normal. After a few deep breaths I try and put back the air of superiority that I normally hold.

"What are you doing here Christopher?" I ask, trying to smooth back out my tone.

My best friend looks at me with confused puppy eyes before saying, "I've come with letters from Commandment," His words get all three of us to lean in closer. "They seem to think that you three are screwing things up here so they've sent me in to fix things," The smile on his face is unnerving in an almost pitiful way. I exchange a look with Bryan and Lea. Its enough to tell that neither of them are pleased by this. "The three of you managed to miss a traitor in your mist and that he got kicked out only two days in. Pictures haven't been taken yet, so I was sent over to take his spot," I can feel my jaw literally drop open and it takes my befuddled mind a minute to figure out how to close it. "There is going to be a tight schedule for the next few days, one of which I am going to keep a close eye on."

Breakfast arrives and a gleeful look appears on Christopher's face, the same one that is there every time he eats. While he digs in the rest of us are left to stare down at our plates in shock. It's very unlike Commandment to give such an honor to someone with a Demerit. Christopher should be pretty much kicked to the curb now that he's on their 'watch list.' That can only mean that he's struck some sort of deal with them in order to be here. When Chris finishes eating all of us stand up along with him because the rest of us haven't been able to eat a thing.

"For the next few days I'll be acting as Commander," Bryan's face chisels its way into the deep scow, that I normally wear, at Chris' next words. "I'll have you two start preparing things for today's executions while Kiera shows me down to the prisoner."

My throat becomes extra thick and I have to swallow forcefully because no matter how cold I've been feeling towards him, he's still about to go see his brother again. Unaware of what's about to happen, Chris leads us all along the open desert and out to the prison. The wind isn't as unforgiving today but it still takes the slave a long time to clean sand away from me. Chris watches and waits somewhat impatiently. He clearly doesn't know that it takes women more time to get things out of our hair. We depart from the other two and make our way to the Doctor's labs. The walk is silent and it's excruciating; normally, it's effortless for us to be able to talk but right now I can't think of a single word to say to him. The elevator clanks as we go down a floor and the awkward air stirs around us. Thankfully, the Doctor meets us as soon as the elevator opens; I'm so relieved that I fear I may hug him.

"Victor Pole," the Doctor says, clutching at at my hand pathetically before turning to Chris. "Soldier Vierlac! I wasn't aware that we'd be having the pleasure of your company."

Chris' lips sneer at the title. "It's Victor now actually."

The Doctor claps his hands together in delight. "So you've take over for Valenzuar."

He only gets a nod from Christopher and you can see the disappointment emanated on his face. "We're here to see the prisoner."

Doctor Moscuwatts accepts the statement without any fuss and he moves on, with all his fat swaying under the white coat, so that he may move to put in the password. We move through the laboratory and I expect Chris to look around in shocked horror but his face stays mutual. On the left, the woman from the other day is gone and I feel a deep pity within my stomach. The Doctor punches more codes on the far side of the white room and Chris scoots back so I can clamber down the stairs before him. Eventually the last of the codes are entered and we come out into the long hallway of cells. Every prisoner comes to their doors in order to see the new visitor and my heart constricts when I see Jason's long, scarred hands just like the ones I pictured wrapped around me last night.

"Good morning Doctor," Jason calls down from his cell. The Doctor moves us all forward and my eyes flick back to Christopher when we stop in front of his brother's cell. His face has a sour expression on it, but I don't think Jason has seen him yet. "What's on today's menu?" His voice is very snarky.

"Mash potatoes mixed with the rat droppings found upstairs," The Doctor says just as jokingly.

"Fantastic!" He replies heartily.

A sly smile creeps up to my thin lips and Jason looks momentarily pleased to have been the one to make me smile. That is until he spots his younger brother who doesn't come into his line of sight until we are moving onto Val's cell.

"Christopher!" Jason's voice comes out strangled.

My mouth drops down from its smile to a line of pity. After all these years of getting to know Chris, I can tell (despite his silence) that there is a battle raging on inside him. Jason moves along to hang onto the bars that adjoin his cell to Val's so that way he may better listen to our conversation. Two figures huddle on the pathetic excuse of a bed that is in all of the cells. Just by looking at Val, it's easy to tell how filthy one night in the cells will make a person. It looks like he's spent the entire night sleeping in the dirt from how thick the layer of grime is on him. Chris reaches out and grabs hold of the cell bars, slamming the door multiple times as if he's trying to break it open. The result is a teeth shattering sound that wakes every prisoner in the hallway. Val sits up, bleary eyed, trying to figure out where he is until he spots the three of us outside his door. He moves in a cat like crawl as he climbs over the girl so that way he won't disturb her as she tries to go back to sleep.

"Chris," He says when he reaches the door. His tone implies that something bad will occur just by having him in his presence. I guess he does have a point though, all morning Christopher has been ruining my day.

"I have come on behalf of Commandment," Chris says in a voice that even sends shivers down my spine. Val clearly looks surprised and his eyes flick to me, asking the same thing that I've been wondering all morning. What kind of deal has he struck with Commandment so that he may be here? "Since you so clearly messed up far to early, Commandment has sent me to fill in your place and oversee any interrogations you undergo. The best interrogator we have has been sent here and trust me, I will enjoy watching her get answers out of you."

My heart drops down to my toes as every eye trains on me, even Jason's. There's a look of triumph on Chris' face that sends a wave of disgust throughout me. Jason looks hurt and Val looks absolutely mortified. It's pretty widely known to everyone that any form of interrogation is my fortay; several times I've helped soldiers with their interrogations who have long since graduated. It's not that I am just known for getting the results I want, I'm the best. Imagine the thing you hate most about yourself is something that is highly valued and feared by quite a few people. My stomach clenches at the thought of torturing one of my best friends. Thinking of all of the vile ways I've hurt people is terrifying, I can't imagine using a single one on him.

"Kieranna, you can't do that to someone!" Jason cries from the cell next door, only having eyes for me.

"That's enough Jason!" Chris growls, speaking to his brother for the first time in years.

Jason snaps his mouth shut but still continues to slightly shake his head at me. I have to take several deep, calming breaths to give myself a moment to wrap my head around this. My head is pounding again, the pain not likely to come to an end, when more of an audience comes in. Bryan and Lea come into the long room and make their way to us with a sour look on both of their faces.

"What is this about letting one of the prisoners live that is supposed to be executed?" Bryan snaps right into Christopher's face.

My eyes flicker over to the little girl for a second and my whole body breathes a sigh of relief.

"She has been chosen to be spared," Chris answers, having an apparent hate for being contradicted.

"For now," I say sweetly, thinking that I've found my way into getting what I need from Val. "Depends on how well the traitor cooperates."

My smile is sickly sweet and I hate myself for saying those words but I must have our acting Commander think that I fully support his decisions in order to get back on Commandment's good side. Chris' face is full of pride but Jason looks like he's seen the most horrific thing he could ever imagine; I don't know which one disappoints me more.

"Atta girl," Chris clasps me on the shoulder.

I try not to shy away from his touch but I can't help it when I do. The hurt is obvious on his features and I can't bring myself to care. Right now my mind and emotions are going haywire and all I want is for this moment in my life to be over.

"You think about this," Chris says, turning back to Val. "We'll be back tomorrow for our answers."

Then he turns around and saunters off towards the door without a second glance back at us. I let everyone else leave behind Chris before I stare at Jason with his eyes locked on mine.

I'm about ready to leave when Jason whispers, "You don't need to do this. It isn't you."

His voice is so sad, gets under my skin and it makes me hate myself even more. "Sadly, it is."

Maddeningly enough, my mind swirls with images the entire execution time. In one, I'm stealing in an Infinitive marketplace, stealing food for an infant with a boy who probably is only a couple years older than me. It's hot, meaning that we are much closer to the desert. Bodies are packed into the tiny square, like peas in a can. My mind tells me that it's maddening to have to squirm my way through the throngs of people. The image so wholly consumes me that I am barely aware of the sand winds whipping through my clothes and hair as the sound of bullets ring though the air as they go in and out of the guns.

My mind shows me Jason more often than not. One scene of him brings faint trickles of tickles to my belly that can only be laughter. The both of us are dressed in rags (me far more grungy than him). I watch him from an alleyway with a touch of pride warming my chest. At some point he comes back to me and waves clutches of blue in his hands. My mind gives me a sense of giddiness to see all of that money.

My eyes soon alert my mind to a change in the events before me and the scenes in my head drift away until I only see the fester before me. Soldiers mill around collecting up the bodies. Apparently one prisoner tried to run because one of our soldiers has to go a ways out to drag the body back in. I thought that I would particularly hate the executions part of the day but the images in my head keep my eyes plenty preoccupied so I didn't have to see it. My ears are still ringing with the sound of gun fire. We are all directed back to the Commander's quarters where we are staying, where photographers wait to photograph the Victors so that people can begin placing their bets on us.

We are forced to take pictures in every situation imaginable. First we take group shots and then we pose in every combination of two that can be though up; which means I had to pose on the arm of every boy. With Bryan I try to squirm as far away from his grasp while still staying within his reach. Lea holds onto me loosely while with Chris I can't stay back into his arms. I stay within the circle of his reach but I can't force myself to lean back into him.

"Commander," The photographer calls over to Chris. He having sent everyone away but me. "I wanted to congratulate you on the promotion. That Valenzuar traitor never deserved it," Chris purses his lips together at the touchy subject.The man studies us rather quizzically before grabbing one of he printed pictures. "You two look rather fetching together."

The man does have a point. There's a certain unity there that does not exist amongst the other pictures. Chris clearly holds me in he circle of his arms loosely but I stay back pressed against his chest, not fighting him like I felt like I was. We both have a strong, unforgiving look about us that is essential for an Oslian Soldier. Together we look unyielding like Commandment should. The picture makes us look that the two that will win.

Chapter Nine

My head is still pounding that next day and my body is riddled with stress, the thought of the upcoming interrogation fills my head. Tactics float through my mind for what this day entails, each thought more terrifying than the last. Every thought makes my head pound harder until I fear my brain may explode from my skull. I twitch there, in pain, as I lay in my bed in the very early hours. Images are flooding through my mind; each and every one of them is more excoriating than the last. Every detail is hazy and I can't make out the details. It's as if my mind is trying to make me feel guilty about what I am about to do today.

Dead bodies are littered all around my feet as I tear through a town in search of something. Eyes rolled back so that I can only see the whites, brings up my gag reflex and I fear I may choke. One of the images has me cornered and I lash out at the man until he is laying in a steadily increasing pool of his own blood. By this time I am withering in bed as my mind continues to show me images of the dead that I have supposedly killed.

At some point a slave comes in to get me ready for the day but she immediately runs out when she sees my agonized features. There's hustling and bustling going on out in the hallway but my mind can't process it because my brain is too busy showing me things that make me hate myself even more. The shaking intensifies until, I think, a wail escapes my lips. That's when Chris comes in. I've just seen myself with Jason, me perched atop him with a knife pressed to his throat, when Chris sits on the bed pulling me into his arms. That's when my body stills, and it's not due to comfort like he thinks because Chris soon starts to croon in my ear.

The images stop for a moment before they take a whole new, startling path. Now I'm in chains, back against a cell wall, cowering there in a blood stained dress. Bryan comes into the room and is gently stroking my cheek until Chris, shockingly, comes in. He's talking to me, but I can't hear any words although fear riddles my body. Soon I am forced to dress in the normal training uniform that I wear at Oslia. I am then etched from my cell by Bryan and Chris, being drug down a hallway that I can now identify as the cells below the Doctor's experimental ward. By now I know the place well enough to know that I am being dragged down to the room that is what the Doctor called "unfit for a lady".

The door is flung open and I am forced into a room that greatly resembles the one upstairs, except this one has one lonely machine in it. The coffin like contraption is just like the very one from upstairs. I am shoved and strapped down to the ugly contraption when Doctor Moscuwatts comes in. He speaks, but the words are still muddled as if I'm hearing them through a wall.

Something is then injected into my vein and instead of blacking out, my eyes shut but the world still goes on around me. Then the pain starts like something is digging into my skull then it stops and the saw starts. The pain is the utmost excruciating thing that I have ever felt. I wish that my head would just explode so that I may be through with the pain. It would feel far more comfortable to bang my head with a hammer. It's like my body is experiencing this for the first time, unlike all of the other images that float through my head. That's when my brain feels as if a needle is digging into the back of my head.

I wrestle my way out of the covers and Chris' arms until I can collapse on my hands and knees in the bathroom. That's where I vomit up anything that is left in my stomach, as waves of pain stab into my brain. Something feels as if its coming and going through the tissues of my brain. Then I scream a blood curdling, awful scream and Chris is once again holding me, attempting to comfort me.

For a brief moment I feel as if I can't remember anything, not even my name, it's just like something is missing. All of the pain is gone. I feel nothing. I know nothing. A black hole that only exists in my head and then it's like everything I know is roughly slammed back inside my mind. Now I lay on the cool tile, gasping, choking on air while I sit in the circle of Christopher's arms. Minutes go by, maybe an hour, as I wait for my stomach to calm down and I am able to stand. Once Chris deems that I am finally well enough to get something done for the day he leaves me. Slaves come to help me dress but I still feel all alone.

I stand in front of the mirror wearing dark blue, flaring pants, a white blouse and boots, looking ghastly pale. My whole figure looking sickly; each step I take to get downstairs wobbles as if I'm on a boat and haven't gotten my sea legs yet. Breakfast is slow and agonizing, all I can manage to eat is a couple bites of toast and nothing else. Today the wind knocks me around in a very vulnerable way. I can practically feel every thump of my brain against my skull as I walk through the drifting sand as I move with my friends and Bryan.

"How long will this take?" Chris asks as I'm getting the last bits of sand cleaned away from my clothes.

"Could be all day," I try to say with as much confidence as I can muster.

Lea and Chris both walk with me as far as the elevators before they leave me to head up to the interrogation chambers as I head downstairs. My descent is slow; its almost somber when the Doctor and some soldiers join me. Every prisoner is silent when I and my entourage enter, all of whom know that we're here for their comrade. For the first time Jason isn't there, waiting for me at the door to his cell, he's against the back wall with his arms folded behind him. The scowl that is on his face is pure torture; I look into his eyes and I remember how awful it felt to be perched above him while holding a knife to his throat. The feeling of betrayal is once again very strong but this time I feel like I am the one to betray him. It's awful! My sickly features must concern him because that strong look of brick in his eyes melts to concern.

"I'm sorry," I mouth to him, regret riddling my body.

I nod to my soldiers and they gather around Val's cell, opening the door so that they may extract him. He's soon out and they put him into chains. My head cocks to the side as I watch him glance back at the girl with a sort of worried look in his eyes.

"Her too," I murmur, hating the way tactics run through out my head.

"No!" Val snarls and he starts to thrash around in guards arms.

"Control him," I snap, getting annoyed that he is causing such a ruckus amongst the prisoners. My soldiers start to put the little girl in cuffs before I bark, "That won't be necessary."

With one brief nod of my head they have the two of them dragged through the door and up the stairs. I angle my body to leave but Jason's hand shoots out from between the bars of his cell, clasping onto my arm. Sparks shoot through my body at his touch; I am instantly riddled with anxiety at this sensation. The both of us share down at our skin that as of now rarely touches. Scenes flood throughout my head and I fear that I may collapse onto my knees. Long lost nights scare me as I feel what it's like to be wrapped in his arms. Time of sorrow as we both clutch at the others hand while burying a friend. Anxiety and worry consume me as Jason brings a little boy towards me; I only feel better when he is deposited in my grasp. Both of my arms are pinned behind me as as Jason pushes through the men clothed in a deep maroon. My breath chokes me as a gun is slowly brought up to my forehead. All thought falls away with my gasps, nearly knocking me back to this morning's insanity.

"There's something terribly wrong with me," I gasp more to myself than Jason.

Jason doesn't seem to notice though because he continues to say, "Think of Metais. He wouldn't want you to do this."

His grip tightens and my mind throws me back until I am looking at the little boy that Jason once placed in my arms. A strong protective feeling surges through me and I rip my arm out of his hand.

"Don't bring him into this," I snarl, both shocking Jason and myself.

My words scare me so much that I slowly back from the room and practically run up the stairs. I'm practically panting by the time I make it up to the interrogation chambers. Both Chris and Lea wait there for me while Bryan is actually inside the room, readying Val for me. As soon as I step into the room I can visibly see the fear that is controlling him. This will be an entirely new experience for me; not only am I interrogating someone I know but it's also someone that knows my skills. Trying to add onto his worries, I shrug out of my jacket and hand it to Bryan, rolling through my muscles as I try to intimidate him. I'm actually able to see his muscles clench tighter as I take a seat in the chair that is positioned in front of him. With a nod from me, Bryan leaves the room to fetch something for me. The two of us stare at each other, both fully aware that cameras are in here for the sole purpose to record our every word.

"This is your last chance to tell me what I want to know," I threaten, my hate for myself is all that I can feel.

He sits there with his lips pressed tightly together, showing me that he won't relinquish a single word.

"Fine, have it your way," I murmur, frustrated this he is going to be this uncooperative.

Right on cue Bryan comes in with a basin filled to the brim with water. Val shrinks back in his chair when he sees the water sloshing around in its container. Having known Val for years has really helped me me dig into his fears and know what controls him. Years ago, his own father was killed in an interrogation by rebels and he was submerged in the water until he choked on it and died floating there. Ever since the Val has been afraid of going under water. It may be unfair to him, since I have had the ability of knowing him so well, I may actually scare answers out of him rather than force. Bryan brings the bowl directly in front of Val, in replacement of my chair, and then goes to stand behind Val. Every time that I interrogate someone, I always have a partner that acts as my muscle so that way I will not waste my strength during the brutality. More often than not, Bryan is the dumb meat standing by my side.

"Why," I start, crouching down in front of Val. "Did you betray your country? Especially after you've worked so hard to protect it."

He just sits there, mutely, acting like he didn't even register my question but I can see the tears in his eyes. Frustration builds inside me and I finally nod at Bryan. Val's head is forced under the surface of the water; he barely has a few seconds of breath. Bryan holds him under by the neck, not relinquishing a millimeter when Val tries to fight his way up. By the time a minute has passed, his body is starting to shake, fighting to consume air. I let myself give him another thirty seconds before having Bryan bring him up for air. I can't be sure but I think that there are tear rapidly falling from his eyes, intermingling with the water from the bucket. As soon as his face breaks through the surface he is coughing up lung fulls of water all over the cool, white flooring and walls, even getting some on me. Anger rushes through me when I take in the mess that he made

"Look what you've done," I whisper into his ear before I back hand him across his face.

My mind shoots me back to an image of being slapped across the face by a soldier many years ago. It takes all my strength to pull myself out of that memory. Once my mind throws itself back into the interrogation, I look at my palm, which is now red, and feel that smarting sting on my own cheek. I must look down at my clothing to once again make sure that I am wearing our country's colors. I'm suddenly consumed with grief, and hate for myself threatens to choke me.

From my place beside Val, nelt down on the floor, I am able to whisper into his ear, "I don't want to do this," I nearly choke on the words, trying to keep my own tears in my eyes. "Something is terribly wrong and I am not certain of anything anymore."

His big, brown eyes flick over to me so that he is able to get a full look at me, so that he may be able to tell if i'm bluffing. Despite that Bryan wasn't able to hear what I said, he knows that I said something not completely sane. With one wave of my hand Bryan is out the door, leaving me and Val alone.

"I can't be certain of anything anymore," I continue on in a hushed voice. "I am remembering things that should never even exist in my mind. People that I have never met but I know that they are real," I can barely manage to say, seeing every image that has controlled me since i got her. "They terrify me. I see them everytime I close my eyes. It's like I lived this whole other life, one that I almost know nothing about. Now I see Chris and Bryan in my memories as terrifying beings when in reality I can control them any way that I want to. The prisoner from downstairs occupies more than half of my thoughts," A look of fear flashes through his eyes and I can't place it.

"Jason tells me all these things but I can never be fully certain they are real. All I know is that I have feelings for Jason that Chris wishes I felt for him," My mind is slowly coming back to itself after getting all of that off of my chest and I am finally able to remember the task at hand. My voice drops down to a purr as my hope for control rises. "Some of my memories are true in an utmost frightening sense. I know what you are thinking," I say, gazing into his eyes. "This isn't right. Any of it. All of it. But unlike you, I am going to do my job and work from the inside to stop this madness. I promise, but now I have to clean up the mess you made here because you never thought it through," I finally whisper before standing up straight and Brian comes in, dragging the girl.

Val thrashes in his chair when he sees her come in. I can tell that he thought I was going to use her all along, just that he wasn't going to have to watch. Bryan drags her to one of the walls that faces Val directly and cuffs her to it.

"Now," I say, trying to return to my normal voice and not that vulnerability that Val heard. "Tell me what I want to know. You betrayed your country; was this girl worth it?"

He stares into my eyes for a while before opening his mouth to speak. "None of this is right," He snarls, repeating the words that I fed to him moments ago. "One innocent life was spared because I took matters into my own hands. A little girl should not die because we are running out of room for her. Madeline should not have died because there was a lack of space to keep her," Val rambles on but I am now looking at Bryan. At this very moment I know that we're both remembering the day that Val had to bury his little sister. "The rebels are right. We shouldn't be living like slaves to Sleisia."

It's like I've unleashed a flood gate inside him because information just rushes out of him. Bryan and I both step outside the room and let the cameras catch the rest of his words. Outside the door Christopher and Lea wait with a platoon of soldiers.

As soon as we are out of the way Chris says, "Go," and a couple of soldiers rush in.

When Chris follows them inside, I am right behind him. They have the girl snatched up in their hands, both of their of their guns pointed at her head.

"What do you think you are doing?" I scream at Chris as he gives the order and the trigger is pulled on her.

Surprisingly, Val and I are not the only ones screaming, Lea screams at the top of his lungs. Profanities flung at Christopher with all of his might. I yell till my voice is hoarse but even the Val and Lea continue. Chris must have had enough of it because he grabs me by the top of my arm and drags me out into the hall, shutting the mayhem behind us. I rip my arm out of his grasp, his touch not giving me the same pleasant tingles that I get when his brother holds onto my arm.

"How could you kill a little girl?" I yell as the other Victors leave the interrogation room with our soldiers.

"You should do well to remember that this is our job!" He exclaims, pushing me back.

The shock from Chris shoving me must register on my face because Bryan looks like he's about to step in.

"You should do better than to ask Commandment for any favors! It's lucky that you didn't get a demerit," Chris yells.

My anger boils within me and I start to make my way back to him but he slaps me across the face, again, sending me backwards. Bryan barely manages to catch me before I completely lose my footing.

"You're one to talk," I say as I spit saliva at Chris' feet. "What deal is it that you made with Commandment so that you are able to be here? How did you get out of that demerit? You should be right where your brother is at but at least he has a little bit of dignity and did something good before ending up here."

I know that I've hit a nerve, bringing up his family like I did, and it's my goal to his this weak spot. His fist comes flying towards towards my face before my brain can even register it's coming. Soon I'm on the floor with a faint cut above my right eye. As I stumble to my feet, I can already tell that it's going to swell shut. I try to bring my fists up to get ready for a fight, just the way that I am trained, but my head is pounding and my vision is spinning. I don't get a chance to redeem myself in a fight though because Chris soon has a hold of me by my collar, pinning me back against the dingy walls. A feeling of fear jolts through my body at the sight of another soldier, towering over me in an alley, the threat of death hanging over me like a veil. Chris must realize what he's doing and he loosens his grip around me. When his hand unclenches, I take my first gasping breath, remembering that I am once again a small, tiny thing that no matter how much training I've had, size always matters.

"Now," Chris says, trying to rope back in his temper the slightest bit. "Do your job and find out the rest of the information I want from the other prisoners!" He snarls with one final breath before leaving.

Bryan and Lea stay standing beside me, pathetically, as if they don't know what to do now. Bryan soon leaves and and luckily Lea isn't too far behind him. I am left by myself, cowering against the wall, trying to regain my composure before I start doing my job again. Bryan drags Val out of the interrogation room and he has an utter anguished look on his face. It takes a lot of effort but I eventually shake off Lea who comes back to fix me up with a medical kit. By the time that I make it back into the interrogation room the dead girl's body is gone. A new prisoner is brought and Bryan, my meat, is back. The two of us work ruthlessly through the day, picking piece by piece at information until I feel satisfied that we can't get any more out of them. They give me so few words. Many of them end up with blood pouring out of them in some fashion but I'm always careful to leave them just barely breathing so that way they will always remember what it feels like to betray their country.

Only one of them gives me any sort of information that would be worthy of bringing up to Commandment. A man, you can tell that he used to be big in stature but due to lacking sufficient amount of food from years of imprisonment he has really gone down in size, tells me of a rebellion that goes on just outside the war front. People have supposedly been escaping there for years and have just started forming a true guard over the last few years. Supposedly, they've been attacking our resources for centuries, only now doing some real damage. He talks reluctantly at first but once I get him going, he spills everything. He was apparently just a lowly soldier in a vast system that operates outside our borders, all the while spying on us for the rebellion. So lowly that he can't even name their commanders; never seen them at a glance either. Apparently, they have divisional leaders that they report to and their leaders report back to the big shot commanders. The way that he talks about these figures, he has such vehement towards them, you may think he was talking about the sun. It startled me to see such loyalty from one of their followers, it'll make it harder to turn a single one of them. The man talks so much that he rambles his way into unconsciousness.

Bryan has just snatched the man up in his arms when I say, "Bring me Jason."

There's a slight fear on his face but he takes my order and follows it all the same. I am left alone, slumped in the chair that I was sitting in at the start of Val's interrogation. By now I feel exhausted, having gone through every prisoner in- what I have now come to call- the traitor cells. My head is pounding and the longer that Bryan is gone, the more I sweat buckets. Time goes by, I don't know how long but it feels like hours, and the pain in my head becomes so acute that i fear I may black out. The door to the interrogation chamber opens and Bryan comes in with Jason who is walking almost civilly beside him. As soon as they see me in my fetal state they seem to stop short. My glare towards Bryan intensifies and he is forced to cuff Jason to Val's old seat, all the while ignoring my severe gaze.

"Leave us," I am barely able to command of him. He starts to leave but doesn't make it all the way through the door before Isay, "And shut off the cameras. I don't want them catching any of this."

Bryan looks concerned but he soon does as I say. I sit there, in pain, watching Jason as he watches me. Counting down the minutes until I hear the familiar click of cameras shutting off. I slink towards Jason, watching his features turn to a disbelieving panic. I am within inches of him when my agonized brain realizes that he thinks I'm going to hurt him. My knees buckle from underneath me and i fall down near his feet. My hands fall on top of the bend in his legs and I can watch as it pains him to not reach out and comfort me.

It's the lack of his touch that finally undoes me when I say in a strangled cry, "What is wrong with me?"
Chapter Ten

I open my eyes to find myself in a white, horrifying chamber. Nothing in here is familiar, not even my clothing. I wear what I can only imagine a female Slesia offlical would wear. Too much black, too many sharp outlines to the outfit that almost make it look painful. My clean, polished hands rest on a man's knees. Jason's knees. A sob chokes out of lips and I reach up to clutch at him with what I thought were weak arms. As soon as I get my arms around his neck I can feel my muscles engage and I fear that I may choke him; disgust for myself shoots throughout my body. I don't know what's wrong with me. I haven't seen Jason since the raid and I basically just attacked him. My sobs threaten to suffocate me even more as I take precautionary steps away from Jason. My chokes come with tingles that press into my head like a billion little knives. Once again I almost hit the floor as I struggle to keep my knees from buckling. Images swirl through my head, images of knives and punches thrown and bullets spewed. Fear courses throughout me and I start to cower back towards Jason.

"What's wrong me with me, Jas?" I ask sobbing, horror rockets through my body as I speak an entirely different language.

His eyes widen into two huge circles and his Jason drops the slightest fraction of an inch.

"Kieranna?" His voice drips like honey when he says my name.

I move over to him, positioning myself on his lap, expecting him to put his arms around me in comfort but when he doesn't my mind starts to swirl even more. My eyes flick down and I see his wrists are chained to the arms of the chair that we are both now in.

"Check your pockets," Jason says when he catches my look of concern.

When I reach into the pocket of my pants, my perfectly shaped fingers brush against metal. I fish the key out and struggle to grasp any sort of control as I unlock him. As soon as I'm finished, his arms come around me and they are skinnier than I remembered them being just yesterday. Everything swirls around me as I take in the differences between us; things that should take months to change has happened in a small twenty-four hours. He takes his nose and nudges along my jawline until his lips reach mine. He breathes me in like this may be the last time he ever gets to hold me. I notice things different, his whole face is thin and when he nudged along my cheek bone, there was an acute pain. When our lips slide across each other's I can feel a jagged scar dominating the left portion of my top lip. We pull away and share one last lingering breath before I lose it. I'm off his lap within seconds and across the room, looking at myself in the giant mirror that dominates half the wall. One of my fingers is raised to tap on it but I get lost at the sight of my reflection.

My hair is braided back in a much longer tail than I've ever been able to do. I notice that by looking at my reflection that I have a black eye that I cannot remember getting. Images are once again swirling through my body, it's all I can do to keep my too perfect nails from digging into my brain to make it stop. The images of a punch thrown directly at me by a man that looks very much like my Jas.It frightens me deep down to my bones, it scares me to see him in even more glimpses. Rain pours down around us but I stay with my body pressed tightly against him as we both clutch at a sword. It's unnerving seeing all these things that I can't remember. I can't even remember how I got to this room; the last thing that I remember is going to sleep in that dark room at the end of the hallway.

Now I'm in a room that I don't recognize, with Jason who I thought had died the day before. Seeing my dead fiancé alive is far more unsettling than my new hair and officials outfit.

"How are you alive?" I ask in that new foreign tongue.

Jason stares at me from the chair as if I'm one of the most peculiar creatures he's seen.

"I was never dead," He answers in a simple maddening way.

"You bled out in my arms," I start to cry, unnerved by my unfamiliar voice.

"No," He says but this time his words shake and quiver.

"Yes," I say, my head fighting against my heart which wants that to have never happened. "You died yesterday!"

My tears are falling steadily as Jason gets up and walks towards me. Stopping a few feet away from me when he says, "Darling, I haven't seen you in seven months."

My world spins and I feel like I'm falling throughout space and time. Nothing in my world makes sense anymore. One of my feet slips and this time i actually am falling. Jas reaches out with both of his hands and clutches at my forearms. Soon I am uprighted on both of my feet, barely able to contain myself. There's a screaming in my head that I can't ignore and a dull ache in the back of my scalp where my body subconsciously knows a scar will be. My claws scrape along me, pulling out locks of my hair until there are patches missing from my braid. Jason sees that I am purposely harming myself and he locks hold on both of my wrists, trapped in between his hands. With my hands trapped, it forces my body to calm down, the pain temporarily subsides but the terror remains.

"Explain," I beg of him.

Jason guides me over to the chair and places me down on his lap after he's taken a seat.

"I don't know what's been happening," He says not even attempting to sugar coat it. "The last time that I saw you was at our wedding but that was seven months ago. Since then I have been stuck in a cell wasting away until you showed up a week ago. Granted you didn't remember me, I never thought that you would regain memories of me again. It's like you've lived this whole other life, one that I had no part of. Something broke you down just a little bit ago. It brought you back to me."

My senses threaten to choke and I can barely hear Jason plead, "Don't leave me."

I'm ready to start crying all over again when he buries his face in my neck and I can feel myself slip away.

Chapter Eleven

My eyes open and the feeling of needles poking into my brain shakes me down to my core. I sit within the circle of Jason's arms positioned securely on his lap, with his face buried deep within my neck. Every muscle in my body immediately clenches up, even the tears that have mysteriously started to fall down my cheeks, stop along their path. I'm frozen, all the warmth leaving my body as I fail to access any sort of memory that brought me to this position. Jason senses my discomfort and he removes his face from my neck. A panic spreads across his features and I fling myself away from his body. Within seconds I am on my feet, as soon as my body loses contact with his I feel a searing hot pain that is stabbing through out my skull. I press both of my palms flat against the sides of my head. The pain is so terrible that I think I may vomit all over the door.

"Kieranna?" Jason asks from his position behind me.

There's that name again, something foreign to my brain but it's similar at the same time. My vision doubles for a second and I think I see myself staring at my reflection in the one way glass. I spin on my heel, pivoting around to see that Jason sits in the chair with his hands in his lap and the chains dangling down the sides of the chair. I pat my pockets for the key only to find that its not there. Not having the cool metal on my person unnerves me. He either had to take it from me or I unlocked him and I have no memory of either. I drop down to my knees and start sobbing in an uncharacteristic way. He's up and out of that chair in a flash and is right in front of me calling my body to his. I'm far too bewildered to pull away from him, everything that is going on is completely foreign to me.

"Where did you go?" Jason softly cries along with me. What is even more strange is hearing a man cry, that's something that I never witnessed before. "You can't leave me," He continues to cry in my ear.

My fear intensifies as my body fights to say close to him but my mind fights to protect itself by staying away. The struggle within my body is so terrible that it feels as if someone is taking a chisel and using it to crack my head open. A cry escapes my lips, and I fear that I may black out again like I did this morning in the bathroom. He yanks me back into him when I try to pull away. The blackness around my peripherals starts to fade as Bryan comes banging into the room after having heard me scream.

He comes in to see what must look like Jason overpowering me. Bryan coms over and pushes Jason so that he slides across the floor and I am laying on the floor all by myself. The blackness starts to come back with the pain as Bryan half drags, half carries me across the floor until I am laying underneath the one way glass. The pain is once again terrible and it's so agonizing it causes me to pull into the fetal position.

"Let me help her," Jason pleas from across the room, once again back in his chair.

I'm now seeing two of him, my body shakes so badly because my mind cannot control its bodily functions. I have to force myself to roll over so that I may vomit onto the wall behind me. Eventually I make myself lay on my back so that my face doesn't lay directly in the sick. The two men are still arguing and in the back of my mind I know that it's strange that Bryan hasn't locked up Jason again. That thought doesn't get explored very long though because the blackness finally returns to suffocate me. There's another murmur and then I am being pulled onto a warm, thin lap. I am pulled up to face level and a tight clutch is held on my shaking body so that only my legs are flapping.

"Relax," A frightened male voice whispers into my ear.

The blackness soon starts to dissipate and I am left with a deep pain in my head. It takes time but bit by bit my pain disappears. It takes much longer than I'd like but soon I'm left with a deep dull ache and a foggy mind. Jason continues to hold onto me even after my shaking has stopped. Even through my fog it startles me to not see Bryan trying to force him back into some cuffs so he can be wrestled back into his cell. The scent that he releases when he breathes both calms and sends shivers through me.

My normal sharp as a tack mind cant comprehend the task of counting the minutes that tick by. I think a surplus of time goes by but I can't be sure. Eventually they get me sitting upright in a chair which does give my lungs more expansion room. A palm is rubbed over the surface of my back and I can really feel Bryan digging into my muscles. Jason now stands in front of me and I can't help but feel a little bit of loss. A portion of my brain soon realizes that my normal interrogations don't take this long, that's when panic races through me. I start to get up but four hands descend on me, pushing me down.

"He needs to go back downstairs," I say breathlessly, trying to fight my way through the bars of flesh. "He's been up here far to long."

I can tell by the look in Bryan's eyes that he knows I'm right but he doesn't want to let me up. He's been acting so weird towards me lately, but I have no idea why. The longer I spend thinking about this, the more it hurts my head and I must force myself to stop. The two of them continue to stare at me quizzically. Eventually I am able to convince then both of them to let me up but they keep a cautionary hold on me. My strength is returning, and with Bryan's help I am able to put cuffs back on Jason's wrists. I'm walking toward the door so that Bryan and Jason can get through, since Bryan has escorted every prisoner that has come and gone, but I stop and look back at them. I notice that Jason doesn't at all look like a prisoner who is leaving an interrogation. When Bryan and I lock eyes, we have one brief moment of understanding. Bryan releases his hold on Jason and comes to stand in front of him with me.

"I hope you don't mind but…" Bryan says before throwing a punch at Jason's nose.

His head snaps back in an uncomfortable angle and you can hear the audible snap of his nose breaking. Blood pours down the front of his face; awkwardly, he reaches up to try and position his nose back in place.

"What was that for?" Jason stammers, trying to wipe some blood away while his hands are still clamped together.

"You understand how this works," Bryan says, moving towards him. "Every prisoner who leaves this room looks like he's gone through hell at her hand. I'm just doing the decent thing and sparing you from the hurt of her doing it."

Jason nods, excepting this before Bryan hits him again and again and again. I cringe as I watch this hurt him and I don't know why but a small part of me wants to rush forward and protect him. When Bryan finishes, Jason lays as a bruised heap on the floor. Bryan and I both have to wrestle him up to his feet and he ends up slumped over my shoulder. As we unglue him from me, I'm glad that I wasn't the one to bloody him up because he would be in far worse shape. The both of us take a hold of his biceps and my hand squeezes around bone. It unnerves me to think of how skinny he is; I don't like it. It takes both of my hands to keep Jason up on my side so that Bryan can open the door. Soldiers wait for us outside the door, and it frustrates me to not even see a fraction of emotion on their faces. Jason and I must look horrendous, but it doesn't shock any of them. It's maddening. The two of us drag Jason out into the hallway that is filled with our inferiors, as his head droops to the side. I'm sure it's all for show but it concerns me. We get halfway down the hallway when my breath becomes heavy due to my previous episode.

"Victor. Ma'am," One brave soldier dares to address me. "Allow me."

His hand is outstretched towards me, an offer that he will soon wish he didn't make. I try to bring myself up to my full height even with a person clutched in between my hands. It must work because his spine slowly starts to shrink in length as if he wishes to not be above me in any way. He looks like one of those wild dogs in the marketplace that runs away with his tail tucked between his legs. This thought startles me as soon as its through my head because I've never been to a market place before. Not even as a little girl, at least I don't think so. Have I? I don't know anything anymore.

"I've got this," I snarl rather roughly in his place. "In fact you're dismissed."

I look pointedly at his chest which holds our country's emblem sewn to his soldier; the same one that is sewn to me. One of the men gasp in surprise (this probably being the first time he's ever seen someone dismissed) but I don't have the time or patience to address it. The soldier in front of me just stares into my eyes before ripping off his patch in disbelief. He then places it in my outstretched palm. I place the patch in my pocket when I know the man is watching then I go back to clutching at Jason with both hands. I have to tug at Jason's body hard, which I hate doing, but I have to get Bryan moving. Once inside the elevator- just the three of us- Jason tries to stand up more on his own so that we don't have to support him.

"You shouldn't have done that," Jason says so quietly that I'm not even sure Bryan can hear him. It seems like all Jason does is tell me what not to do.

"I should have. And it doesn't matter," I say hotly.

"Think of his wife and children. Think of the shame this will bring him. I know it will. It should matter because now his loved ones may leave him because they will think he's a nothing."

My already sullen mood worsens, "That is no concern of mine."

"But it should," Jason gives me one last murmur before slumping back into Bryan's and mine arms so that we can exit the elevator.

Many soldiers wait for us as we exit the elevator and they surround us as we drag Jason down the flight of stairs until we reach the Doctor's labs. Doctor Moscuwatts starts along after us with what I believe to be open shock. The password to go down the stairs is put in, something that I still don't know, then we drag him down. The platoon of soldiers wait at the stop of the stair as we place Jason in his cell. The metal groans open just like the rest of the prisoners who lay in the cells in pain. We place him on the thing that barely passes as a mattress and I've just unlocked him from his bindings when he catches my hand. He clutches at me pathetically, and I can't help but have my cheeks blush and my heart melt at the soft pressure of his skin against mine.

"Come back to me," He whispers just before bringing my knuckles to his lips.

For some reason I don't think he means to come back just for a visit. He wants me; something he's missing, to come back.

"I will, Jas," I promise.

The shock is on both of our faces, I feel as if I called him that nickname out of habit.

Chapter Twelve

My trudge back through the desert is lightly border line pathetic because Bryan has to keep a firm hold on me. Ever since we left Jason my stamina has been steadily decreasing and my will to continue is waning. By the time we make it to the door of the small house we're living in Bryan has to wrap an arm around my waist to almost carry me up to my room. The door to my chambers is opened for us and it shocks me to see Chris there waiting for me. The three of us stand there staring at each other for a moment that feels like it will never end. Finally, Christopher grabs my arm roughly and pulls me inside while I still have Bryan hanging onto me. The door to my office is slammed shut as soon as Bryan and I fully enter the room.

"Sit," Chris growls as he takes my seat at my desk.

Both of us do as we're told and take the seats across from him.

He sits there fuming for a while before he finally starts to chew us out, "Why the hell did you turn off those cameras?" His spit flies until it hits my face and I must resist the urge to wipe it off. "You have no authority to do something like that. "You have no authority to do something like that. All that data is now lost because the two of you decided to be stupid."

"With all due respect, Commander," Bryan retorts with an all to sarcastic growl. That even right now, I even know that it's not the right time to try to be Alfa. "We did you a favor. Would you really wish to watch your older brother, who betrayed his whole country, get tortured by the women you claim to have feeling for? But that doesn't even seem right because you struck her fourteen hours ago."

Both of them sit there almost growling at each other; both not wanting to let the matter drop. I feel very stuck in between the two even though the conversation includes me.

"What may or may not affect me is no concern to you. And as your Commander what I say goes. You should be very glad that I am not giving your ass a demerit purely for talking back."

Bryan leans even further forward in his chair and I am starting to feel increasingly more exhausted by their debate. My mind is once more becoming cloudy and all I can smell is the rustic scent of other people's blood on my clothing.

"You're only the Commander for a few days!" Bryan shouts, slamming his hand down on the table as he stands. Chris rises as well so that way he can match Bryan's height. "Need I remind you that you were not one of the originally selected like we were? If anything we had the right to but you most certainly don't have the right to stand above us and lecture us like children."

They stay there staring at each other for another minute before Chris storms out of my office. My eyes widen slightly in shock, but far too exhausting to do anything else. We sit there for a few minutes in silence until I decide to move over to my seat. The cushions are still warm but I can't bring myself to squirm at this awful feeling. There is once again a deep throb in my head that makes me wish I was again being comforted by Jason. My head flops back against the back of my chair and it's all I can do to not succumb to the mist in my mind. For a brief moment I see the look of alarm on Bryan's face before he's on his feet, scooping me out of my chair.

The way his steps rock me gently as he carries me over to my bed in the next room is comforting. He places me down on top of the duvet and I am able to soak into the foamy mattress. A cover is pulled over me while I'm still wearing my bloody clothes and shoes. That's the last thing I know.

I finally fall into the depths of my mind and this time I feel comforted. A gathering of people, including Jason, are smushed around a table, all focusing on a pathetic piece of a map. There is a great deal of irritation coursing through me as I attempt to argue with them. Jason stands across from me, smiling back arrogantly as he himself argues with me. It's beyond frustrating and I can't help but stick my tongue out at him. Everything's so agitating that it brings on a whole new memory that's even more irritating. I'm standing at a doorway and somewhere nearby there are crashing waves that ring in my ears. Three people are in the room next door and I'm just barley listening to them as I open the door. Outside Jason stands there in the brutal sun, his too thin skin turning slightly pink.

We stay there, looking at each other for several long moments. Moments far too long considering how long it's been since we've last seen each other. I step outside the door so that I may throw my arms around him but as the same time I step forward, he steps back. For a second I'm hurt. I don't understand.

"What's wrong?" I know my lips form the words.

He fidgets there, not doing anything but stirring circles in the sand with his boots.

"This isn't working," I hear his next words through a fog. I'm hearing it but not comprehending it. "I can't even begin to describe how much I care for you but I'm gone all the time and I can't ask you to come with me. You'd be losing to much."

Deep in my mind I know this makes no sense because I have nothing to lose. He reaches out and tries to grab one of my dangling hands but they fling back out of his clutch. My mind is able to see through my eyes, my emotions detached. As I watch him leave I can't help but notice the look of hurt on his face.

The scene once again changes and I'm standing in the marketplace with a boy that can't be older than five clutching at my hand. A desert fruit staining my hand with its purple skin. Something across the dusty streets catches my eye and I follow it through the clinging dirt.

Jason stands there, almost like he's watching me but he soon slips away down the alley. I hand the fruit to the little boy and pass him into the arms of another girl standing beside me. Slinking through the densely packed streets, I try to make my way through the crowd. I eventually make it to the alley and I can just barely make out his silhouette that is steadily moving away from me. A man follows behind me, Im sure of it, and the emotion that I experience is not fear but pure annoyment. I carry on down my way despite my stalker. Eventually I exit out alley and spot Jason walking a ways down in the think crowd. I'm about to go out after him, but the man behind me snatches ahold of my waist. When I turn around I am not at all surprised to the man who holds onto me.

I push my way out of his grasp and snap, "What're you doing here?"

"Trying to keep you from making another mistake," The man answers rather snarkily. "Jas already told you to leave him alone."

My eyes mist over at the reminder and I'm just able to catch his movement as he disappears into the crowd. I turn back around to face the brown eyed teenager and I can tell that he was following Jason's movements just like I was.

"I have to know why," I can barely make myself say.

The boy looks back out into the sea of people then he grabs my hand and pulls me into the throng, guarding me with his long body. We move along behind Jas, always keeping a good distance. He pulls off the strip of people moving into their homes for the night and down another alley way. A few more turns later and we're behind some of the richest house in the Oswana District, just on the outskirts of the Oslia Soldiers Head Training Quarters. For some reason, my body is a live wire at the thought of being so close to so much money. It makes my hands itch at all the temptation to take it.

The three of us, Jason not knowing we're here, stop not far from the train tracks. The brown haired and eyed boy places his arm out in front of him so that I'll stop, even if it means me running into him. We don't wait there long, barely any time for me to watch Jason as we hide in the shadows. Lights are soon reflected back into us from the North and I have to squint my eyes to see the oncoming train. For a second I fear that Jas may see us from where me and the boy hide but the train soon buzzes by in front of him. Hands are reached out from one of the cars and they pull Jason inside. I would be shocked if it hadn't looked like he was waiting for them. The front of the tain is getting further and further away until its only the last few cars are buzzing by. The fear of being left behind starts to course through me and I start run after it, the boy not following me.

"Wait, Kieranna!" The boy yells out to me.

I don't even bother looking back, I'm barely able to reach a boxcar with its door open and before I know it, I've launched myself inside. My left slide slams into the hard metal and down into my hip bone there's an ache. Soon the boy is on the car beside me and I'm standing up, rubbing my hip as I survey the medical supplies. Next thing I know, Im cowering in the corner of the train car with the boy in front of me. Hands are reaching into the open car, pulling out the supplies that for the time being are hiding our existence. Im shaking as a man steps onto the car, tossing all the crates to someone else. The boxes are leaving quickly and the man eventually spots the boy in front of me that hides my tiny frame.

"What're you doing here? You shouldn't be here!" The man screams at the boy who presses himself tighter against me.

More people come and pull him away as he fights to stay with me. They practically throw him off the train like he's part of the supplies. A tiny yelp escapes my lips and that sound draws their attention back to my corner. Several people exclaim the word "hey" and hands reach out to catch me. I dodge the first two and scurry to the door which I jump out of. I land on the opposite side of the train that they threw the boy out at. I hit the compact earth in the smoldering heat and almost immediately, am spotted by a few men. I start to run in the direction of the train but it's way to easy for them to catch hold of my scrawny arms. I fight and kick at them but the more I struggle, they just lift me up between them. They carry me all the way around the train to the spot where they have the boy bound and gagged. I'm tossed down beside him and someone comes to tie me up. I can tell what we look like to the people who have captured us; dirt caking us, both too far underweight. Two people eventually come and scoop us up by our collars. The whole time i try to apologize to the boy but it may not come out as meaningful with my gag. We are pulled this way and that until we are led just outside a building where a group of people stand in a big circle.

"Sir?" The man who has hold of me tries to get the attention of someone in the gathering. One of the men turns around and it startles me to see that it's Jason. It's clear that he's surprised to see us because his eyes look like they may bug out of his head. "We found these two hiding out in a supply car. Seems like these two Infinitive were trying to rob us."

I roll my eyes at this man's stupidity; it's obvious that even Jason thinks this guy is a moron.

"What are you doing here Kieranna?" Jason asks looking right at me.

I bite down on my gag and make a big point of mumbling unintelligible words through the cloth. Jason takes one of his hands and drags it down his face, I've barely been here a couple minutes and I'm already annoying him. He flicks his fingers and the cloths are ripped out of both our mouths.

"Thought you would have been able to stop her, Sebastian," Jason says, now focusing his attention on the boy beside me.

Deep down I always knew that was the boy's name but it still surprises me to hear it.

"I tried," He mumbles. "But when she started to follow you, I couldn't let her go on her own."

Jason closes his eyes for a second as if this physically pains him. I desperately want to say something so that I can defend myself but trying to do so would only result me getting yelled at by Jason and the boy, Sebastian.

"So did the two of you just leave Metais behind?" Jason asks, giving both of us a rather disapproving look.

Sebastian's head hangs low in shame and by now I can't help but interject.

"Isn't that what you did to us?" I snap. His eyes widen a bit more and I should feel bad for snapping at him but its the truth. He shouldn't be shocked by me getting mad at him, he should know by now that I have a bad temper."And for your information… we did not leave them. We're obviously going back to them, that is if you'll even let us."

Jas rolls his eyes at me in annoyment, even he can't put up with my sarcasm. He flicks his fingers again and we are pulled up to our feet with our bounds still on. That's the last thing that I remember before I fall asleep.

Chapter Thirteen

I wake up and blankets are twisted around my legs. There's sweat slicked all over my body and I can just barely remember anything about my dream. I have two new names and one recurring one. Sebastian. Camilia. Metias. I drag myself up and out of my bed until I am sitting in my office chair. I can't help but think about when I was last in my office. There's a soft knock on the door and I don't even have a chance to answer before Lea comes in.

"Chris wants to see you in Commander's office," His voice is irritated but he doesn't wait for my response before he leaves.

I smack my head back against the leather of my chair in frustration. I feel like I've dealt with Chris enough to last a lifetime. Eventually I am able to get up and get going. I have to go up an entire another level in the house so that I can reach the office. The Commander has an entire floor all to himself and everyone else is expected to remain downstairs. Outside the door Bryan leans up against the wall as soon as I get closer he looks over at me.

"So you got called here too?" I ask him, suspecting that both of us are in trouble from our earlier conversation with Chris.

"Seems like it. Lets go," He says begrudgingly before open up the door.

Bryan and I both take a seat across from Chris in the Commander's office in the prison. It's been a while since I've sat in this office but I've never been in here as a guest. Chris sits in the big chair, totally ignoring us as we wait for him to finally acknowledge why he needed us here so promptly. Finally, he looks up but when the moron does, he just stares at us. The man that I once thought I knew, really has a thing for dramatics. His stare is so annoying, it feels like his eyes are digging into my skin.

When he finally decides to speak, his words have nothing to do with me. "There is a woman up in the prison cells in the capital who Commandment thinks may know the leader of the rebellion," He pauses, waiting for a reaction from either of us but when none comes he continues. "They think that she may have the correct names to give us."

In my head I know that this is a big deal but I can't bring myself to care or even ask why I should.

"What does that have to do with us?" Bryan asks after a few awful moments of silence.

Chris drags both his hands down his face in exasperation, as if its paining him to have to talk to us.

"A team needs to be sent to interrogate her and our best team is here," Chris sound exasperated.

We all know that the best interrogators are here and they're sitting right in front of him.

I purse my lips as I nod. "When do we leave?" I ask, a million different scenarios running through my head.

"Tomorrow," Chris answers simply. Bryan nods and gets up to leave and I start to follow after him but

Chris stops me. "Wait, Kiera," He calls as soon as my hand is on the door knob, going to close him inside the vast room.

I slowly turn back around and I'm commanded to come take a seat across from him. Our silence us one of the most awkward things I've ever felt, especially with him sitting there, staring at me. Soon he's up out of his chair and moving around so that he's able to take the seat the Bryan was just in. I try to do my best to scoot away from him but when I try to he reaches out and grabs hold of my thigh. There a knot in my throat and I must resist the urge to throw up.

"I don't know why you keep resisting me," Chris says, pulling me towards him by my leg.

All my muscles tense up as it takes all of my willpower to not pull away, "I'm not," I barely whisper, trying to appearance that i'm not cowering.

All of my lessons of not refusing superiors runs through my head as I try to not squirm away. To back away now would make me seem like a coward, not something that would help my case right now.

Randomly, one of his hands reaches up to gently touch my cheek and play with my hair. That's when I finally jump to my feet and back away towards the door. Chris' expression is a weird mixture of anger and shock. Im careful to not turn away from him but rush out the door while I'm still facing him. Only when I'm out in the hallway do I collapse with my back against a wall and take in gasping breaths.

Chapter Fourteen

That next day I force myself to go through the usual motions of my daily routine. People come to clothe me and different slaves come to pack my belongings that I will be taking to the capital with me. Soon I am decked from head to toe in our country's colors. I am swathed in blue pants that swish along the tips of my black heels when I walk and a crisp white blouse. Once Im clothed, I go and lay face down on my bed, pressing my forehead into the pillows, just trying to forget my memories from last night. It doesn't help but it does give me something to do until Bryan comes to get me. He basically has to force me out of my sanctuary and into the hallway.

Our trudge is slow and the noise from my heels on the floor is almost too much for my head. Click. Click. Click. Sounds as if my brain is slamming itself against the lining of my skull. When we reach the downstairs level, we go past one of the Commander's offices and we are just able to see two men sitting in there. At first glance I thought I was wrong but when I'm back tracked, it stuns me to see whos in the room. Two brothers sit across from each other, the younger on in the seat of authority. Jason and Chris. Chris spots me first and scowls to see that I've witnessed their meeting. If anything he should have known better than to leave the office door wide open.

"Kiera," Chris snaps.

Jason immediately turns around in his seat when he hears my name.

"Just the two idiots I was needing actually," His voice dripping with sarcasm when he sees that Bryan is with me.

Bryan comes to stand behind me and there is some hidden emotion that flashes across Jason's eyes. Both of us take a few steps inside the room only stopping when Christopher holds up his hand; we oblige to his wishes just this once.

"I trust that you two are ready to ship out?" He asks so that way it's almost not a question but something that he expects.

"Yes commander," Both of us grumble in a mocking way.

Chris stares at the both of us for a minute, irritated that we would give him that title out of mockery. Eventually he stands and focuses his attention on Bryan.

"We need to discuss a few things about your assignment," Chris barks, walking out the office door. Both of us turn to follow him out the door, but he stops me. "Just Bryan. You stay and watch the prisoner."

The two of them leave, shutting the door in my face, stunning me. I am shell shocked, my thoughts spiral, my overactive brain conjuring up scenarios. Each one more wild than the last. As of this minute my skills surpass both of theirs, I should outrank the both of them.

"Kieranna?" Jason asks and I whirl around to face him, a wild look in my eyes.

I know that i'm not hiding my emotions at all and that frightens me even more. To have my fears and emotions on full display while i'm at a weak point, it makes me vulnerable.

"Silence." I snap back, my demeanor trying to compensate for something that I should be able to control but I can't right now.

I want to reach up and yank hand fulls of my hair out, just like the little girl in the psych ward, just to relieve some stress but I can't with my hair being twisted up elaborately. Many deep breaths later, I am promptly up against the door frame with my arms folded against my chest, trying to take up the pose that any normal guard would. My companions are out in the hallway so long that the pain in my head allows my mind to remember things. Right now the pain is so bad that all I can think of is two names. Sebastian. Metias. I stare at Jason, when I should be trying to focus on why he's up in the Victor's house but I can't. All I can think of is the names that are running throughout my head. I feel as if my thoughts are all over the place lately.

"Who's Sebastian?" I randomly ask Jason.

His eyes flick over to me suddenly, it seems like he was just caught up in his thoughts as I was.

He looks at me for a long moment before responding, "He's your cousin. You two grew up together. You actually lived together when you were homeless."

It takes me a second to wrap my aching brain around that. All of a sudden I have some sort of a family and Jason returned that back to me.

"Metais?" I decide to ask next.

This time when Jason looks at me his expression is full of pity and sadness. As if he can't believe I wouldn't know who this is.

"He's your younger brother. You once said that you and your brother had one thing in common that wasn't blood; your father ran out on both of you. Your father abandoned your mother before you were born and had a child with another woman many years later."

I stand by the door, considering this. Suddenly I have what I assume is a little boy that I should be looking after. My chest hurts all of a sudden and I want to cry in loss. I didn't notice before, but I can feel a deep hollow emptiness inside of me. I want to ask him about the girl but the door opens behind me before I can. I side step out of the way and put my soldier facade back on. Chris gives me a look of approval before turning back to his brother. It's like he all of a sudden remembered there was a prisoner in his office and that he was left in the room with me.

"The two of you are dismissed," Chris takes his seat back across from his brother.

I want to turn back around and find out why a prisoner is in our living quarters but Bryan drags my arm and pulls me out. The last thing I see is a sad look from my Jas.

The transport that comes to take us to the capital is far different from the one that brought us here. We are ushered onto the craft and placed into plush seats. Capital slaves come to care for us, first whipping away any traces of sand. Drinks are shoved into our hands as soon as we are gliding through the air. I lay back against the cushions, trying to convince myself to relax but I can't. Bryan sits there, staring out the window, watching as the desert glides underneath us.

"What were you and Chris talking about?" I ask him, staring down at the amber liquid in my glass as it rocks back and forth.

He looks over at me with slight sadness, it's as if he knows something that I don't. Even his expression makes me sad.

"He was telling me why a prisoner was in the house," He says into his drink.

My eyes flutter for a second, I can't quite figure out why I couldn't have been there when Chris talked to Bryan. If he just needed someone to guard Jason he could just have called on any other soldier.

"So what did he say?" I ask, my fingers tracing along the grey fabric of my seat.

"Another interrogator is coming to question the prisoner tomorrow. Chris was trying plea one final attempt to find out what information we got out of him yesterday."

"Oh," Is all I can think of saying.

I don't understand why they would need another team to come into interrogate him. We could have worked on him ruthlessly throughout the night and gotten all of the information that he wanted. It's not like a better team was needed, they already had the best one there. True that we didn't get to much out of him but if we couldn't then no one else could. The woman up in the capital may be important but if she was that important then she would've been shipped to the prison. If anything, we could have interrogated him (again) after we got back. Obviously we are wanted away from the compound and I don't get why. Christopher must have figured out that something is going on with me. That could make me look like an unloyal soldier. It may seem like I'm defecting. That could be punishable with a demert or imprisonment. Jason better keep his mouth shut about anything that I've told him. If he says anything he will be in far worse shape than any insignificant interrogator could do.

As soon as we land in the capital I have to shake Bryan awake, unlike me who couldn't sleep a wink. My mind was a buzz with possibilities that might have happened back at the compound and what will happen to me. Both of us make our way out of the craft and step down into the winter chill of the Capital. Snow litters the ground of Kheross' as we stamp through it to a car that is waiting for us. Slaves place our bags into the trunk and Bryan guides me into the car before sliding in with me. The warmth is comforting and it takes the slight edge off but not by much. As we buzz through the streets I can't help but wonder if I actually lived here. From what I know, I think that I was born here and lived here with my parents until I was six. We were very wealthy, even more so since we could live in the rich sectors of Kheross. To be honest I don't even know if I actually had siblings. I was told that my father and older brothers all died fighting off rebels. My mother died soon after giving birth to me, I was cared for by whoever was home or by servants. Being back in the capital makes me wonder what their lives were like when we lived here, if I lived here. Would they have eaten at the bakery we just passed? Did my brothers petrol these streets before being shipped out to fight? Did my mother shop at the antique stores we drove by? I stare out the window now, wondering if this elte class that we go by may contain people who my family knew.

I've been so stupid lately, questioning things that a prisoner is telling me and letting it get to my head. This whole time I've been thinking two different things, but I know that what is my past and my history. I've let some rat who betrayed his country mess with me until I may have totally killed my life. I've created this mess for myself just because I listened to someone who is less than dirt. Now I have to fight my way up again until I am the utmost feared woman in Oslia.

"You used to live here, correct?" Bryan suddenly asks me.

I nod briefly before deciding to say, "Yes. My family is buried somewhere near here."

He nods his head, thinking about it, "Do you know where?'

"No, I was far too young to remember their funerals," I think of how odd it is that I've never been back to see their graves; I've never once come back to visit home. "I've haven't been back here since I went to Oswana."

I laugh shakely, thinking of how strange it is that I haven't been home in the last fourteen years. I should have connections to all sorts of places here; a training center that I should remember. Something should pop p as memorable but nothing does.

Our car stops in front of our capitals penitentiary We are unloaded and soldiers are at the door to greet us. Soon we are ushered inside and shown up to the elevators. As we go through the lobby I can't help but marvel over how grand everything is in Kheross. Even in the penitentiary everything looks vastly expensive. The whole lobby is decorated in gold, one last wonderful thing for a prisoner to see before being led away to be pumped. My fingers trail along the finely embroidered chair as we pass along to the elevator. Inside is even magnificent, I can't help but imagine what our palace must look like. It's only a few miles away. If this is what a prison in the capital looks like, what must the Emperor's home look like?

When we step out of the elevator I can see the grandeur slip away. The walls change so that there are zero tapestries and everything is covered in a pristine, white color. Colors that remind me of an interrogation floor; the white tile makes it easy to wipe away blood. As soon as we step out of the elevator we are swarmed by even more soldiers. I don't understand the need for all of the security but then I spot him. A young man, not much older than Bryan or I, standing right in the middle of a blue sea. Freckles adorn his strong, serious face. My blush deepens as I let my eyes admire how simple but grand his finely cut suit is. Even through the thick layers of silken fabrics, I can just barely see the outline of sharp, clean, masculine muscles. The elevator shuts and his bright green eyes catch hold of mine from underneath his freshly cut, dark red hair. Our Emperor.

My heart is now stammering hard against my rib cage and I struggle to snap up in salute, not quite sure if that's more appropriate than a bow, considering he is our nation's royalty. I can feel from beside me that Bryan is just as shocked as I am.

"At ease, Victors," A warm husky voice falls from his lips.

I let my arm flop down until it is hanging at my side. The emperor just spoke to me. My brain is at a total loss. I have no idea what to say. He starts to make his way to us, his pack of guards moving with him. When he reaches us his hand reaches forward to clutch at mine. He presses a feather like kiss on my knuckles and for a second I wish that I wasn't wearing the maroon gloves that I used to protect my hands from the cold.

"Emperor, sir," I stammer, struggling to breath.

Our emperor laughs, still holding onto my fingers. "You may call me Ingram, Victor Poll."

My heart stammers through another beat, forgetting the task at hand. Emperor Ingram Nate Derricks just said that I could call him by his first name.

"Likewise, sir," I breathe and then blush, realizing how stupid I must sound. "I mean you can call me Kiera."

Ingram laughs with me and gives my hand a squeeze before saying sweetly, "I understand."

Our laughter soon stops and he releases my hand; I instantly my hand feels colder. He's moved on to talk to Bryan now and I can tell that Ingram has already charmed him. No wonder our Emperor has such good support from our military.

"I hope both of you don't mind," He says now talking to both of us. "I've come to watch you work," My eyes widen at the thought of such an honor. Bryan even hits my arm slightly to make sure I heard him. "Your interrogating skills are somewhat of a legend throughout our country. I was hoping to witness them first hand."

My cheeks are now a brilliant red and Bryan and I respond at the same time, "Of course, Ingram."

There's a slight restricting feeling in my chest when I realize that I called the Emperor by the name that he requested and Bryan by his title. The feeling instantly goes away though when he flashes me a brilliant white smile that is all teeth. Ingram holds an arm out to me and

I take it gratefully. With most men I would have punched them by now for offering my arm but not this time. It must be his class that stops me. Ingram guides us to a door and we are shown inside. I am expecting an interrogation chamber, but it is in fact a viewing room. Once again I feel stupid, there is no way they would have the emperor in the same room as a prisoner without at least a dozen guards. Only a few soldiers follow us in and the emperor pulls out a chair for me in front of the one way glass. I am grateful for the dim room so that way Ingram can't see how flattered I am. He takes a seat next to me and Bryan remains standing behind us. I now know that it is time for me to get to work so I focus my attention on the girl in the chair, only separated by bullet proof glass.

"Camilia Reyes," Ingram says, once again taking hold of my hand. I now know the face name of the girl my dream.

Chapter Fifteen

"Take all the time you need to study her," Our emperor says with a squeeze of my hand.

I know this girl or may have known this girl, either way, something about this girl is familiar. Her arms are cuffed behind her back as she leans forward slightly in her chair as if she's broken. There's this sadness about her that is undeniably loss, she's missing somebody. She's hunched due to the loss of someone's presence. If I only knew who then I'd be able to exploit her in some way. From all the scars on her body I'm guessing. She may be impervious to short term pain. Long term on the other hand may crack her slightly. Going in one by one may not be useful this time, if we go in together then she may gravitate towards one of us. From there I can tell if her lossed one is male or female, from there I can guess what the person might mean to her.

"I think," I start to say to Bryan but soon the whole room is listening to me. "We should start by tying a bar underneath both of her armpits, tie her legs together so she can't kick at us, and suspend her from the ceiling by the bar. It'll give her a pitched forward feeling that will always make her think she's about to be dropped."

Our emperor orders one of his soldiers to be what we need before saying, "That's a very interesting approach," Ingram stares at the girl with open curiosity. "The last interrogator tried hanging her by her ankles and then questioning her."

I desperately want to laugh at this but I settle for a smile. When I look back I can tell that Bryan wants to laugh as well because he smiles just as broadly.

"In my experience that doesn't always work," This once again draws the attention of the whole room, especially Ingram's which gives me a small thrill.

"Why's that Kiera?" Ingram asks me and there's a flutter in my chest to once again have his full attention on me.

There's something personal about having our leader say my name, not just calling me a soldier. Something like warm butterflies flood through me as I stare back into his emerald eyes.

"Well all the blood goes to the head, right?" I ask as if I'm an interrogating instructor. When he nods I continue. "So a few to hard punches and all they can do is cough up blood. You can't really get to much out of them when they're choking on blood."

He laughs and the sound is so infectious that I can't help laughing as well, though I'm drop dead serious. Bryan although stays impartial the whole time, his face as serious as rock.

When we stop he asks me, "What will your first approach be?"

This question makes me want to laugh all over again. It amuses me because I've already thought about this.

"See how hunched and broken she looks?" When Ingram nods, I continue. "She's missing somebody, either they're dead or she was taken from them. Either way, I'll use that person to exploit her."

"Brilliant!" Our Emperor exclaims suddenly in a way that almost makes me jump, and I'm not a jumpy person. "This is why they call you the best," And he reaches out squeeze my knee, making my breathing erratic again. "I'll leave the two of you to work now."

I know that is my que to leave but even as I get up, I struggle. I realize that I don't want to leave Ingram presence. His eyes follow me all the way to the door where we both stop and turn to salute him.

"I'm sure I'll see you afterwards," He says with one last charming smile.

Just when my heart is about to jump out of my throat, we leave.

We enter the room together to see her dangling from the ceiling like meat set out to dry. Her eyes flick to both of us, through swollen slits, when she hears the door open. The soldier who last had his hands on her really messed her up. I can tell that she can just barely see us, her eyes roam over us and at first she flinches away like we are just another pair of soldiers here to pummel her but when she sees my size is considerably smaller, she doesn't quiver as much. She tries to make out our faces but I know she can't. There's blood clotted around the meatballs that are her eyes and I can't help but let my eyes flick back at the glass. I know that Ingram is watching this whole thing and I can't help but wonder if he watched the other interrogator do his work. I highly doubt it though, this technique is so sloppy that I don't think he would have let this happen. That soldier is lucky that this girl is still alive otherwise there would have been hell to pay for killing as asset before needed information is extracted.

My heels click on the blood stained tiles as I make my way towards the girl; for one brief, petty moment I worry that the red is staining the bottoms of them. My piece of muscle meat stays behind though so that way we can at least attempt to figure out who her missing person is. Her eyes follow me, attempting to figure out why my size is so different.

"You're a woman, aren't you?" She asks when I'm within ten feet of her.

"Yes," I say, startled to have a prisoner address me this way. "You are very smart. Even for someone who must have grown up without certain necessities you can guess that I'm a girl because of the clicking of my shoes."

The girl, Camilia, smiles. "It was actually your smell. None of the men that have come in seem to care to shower or spray cologne."

I think about this for a second. This girl is for more intelligent than I originally gave her credit. This does not surprise me at all, my brain seemed to be prepared for it in fact.

"Then I assume you know why I'm here?" I ask, desperately hoping that she wont know the answer.

"I don't actually," She says and a little buzz of thrill zips through me to have beat her. "You're the first woman to enter my cell."

I purse my lips at this, of course I am, I'm the only woman in our military.

"Obviously," I say with a slight chuckle. "I'm the first and only woman that has served for our country."

She smiles slightly and I can just barely make out the fact that one of her front teeth is missing; they're in bad shape as well, almost all yellow. The last person who had his hand on her must have been a real bone head.

"So you're the torturer the whole nation fears?" She asks in an almost nonchalant way for such a gruesome sentence.

I can't help myself but to smile back at her slightly. The whole nation doesn't sound so bad.

"Interrogator," I correct her feeling slightly territorial.

"Ah," She says as if she's trying to understand this. "So do you expect me to just give you information?"

I smile sweetly at this ridiculousness, she's now given me the gender of her lost one. She has failed to speak to Bryan yet.

"Not at all," My smile getting sickly sweeter. "But I would imagine that your arms are starting to hurt by now."

She twitches as if just now realizing this. She's good at ignoring pain until someone mentions it.

"You must be hurting by now. Want me to let you down?" I ask, testing her.

Camilia tries hard to furl her face at me but she's so swollen that she can't. "I don't want to play your games."

I smile, this girl will be a challenge for me, one that I'm going to enjoy. No wonder they needed me out here but I have no kind of information she holds that could be so important. As soon as I start thinking about why I'm here, it leads me down a path that guides me to Jason. My smile falters slightly as I wonder what his interrogator is doing to him. I try to push my grin back on my lips as I push the thought of him out of my head.

"Is that what you told her?" She flinches, knowing that I'm about to begin. As does Bryan, with one flick of his wrist a knife is out and he comes to stand beside me. "Who was she?" My words striking a nerve. "A friend? Family?"

My smile broadens, she reacts differently to the word family there's a deeper pain there.

"What happened to her? Did she die?" Each time I ask a question, the closer I get.

By this time I'm right by her face and gently petting her blonde head. She shrinks away, all the while knowing that I'm playing with her.

"Tell me about her," I say as there's a huff from behind me, Bryans getting a little tired of my games.

"She," The prisoner starts, choking on her sobs, by this point I'm even tired of my games. "She was taken from us. A raid came through the church we were in. A wedding. Her wedding."

This raid, what is with this raid? Everything leads back to this raid and when I look back, it looks like Bryan's jaw is tightening.

"There was a lot of gun fire and smoke. Most of us, we didn't make it," She's crying harder now and Bryan is even more irritated.

I know that he's thinking we'll never get information out of her when our informant is blubbering.

"Who was this? Friends or family?" She nods, giving me confirmation so I can continue. 'Were they rebels?" She nods again. "What were a bunch of rebels doing at a wedding?"

I wait impatiently and I'm about to ask Bryan for the knife before she answers, "They were getting married. Our founders. Our leaders."

My mind buzzes slightly, Jason, Jason was to be getting married at the raid. He's one of the rebels leaders and that woman, Jason claims that I am that woman or that I was.

"And that man, Jason?" I ask her, Camilia's whole body perks up at the mention of his name. "He was taken correct?" She nods slightly and I know that I've found my way in. "What if I could tell you that he's alive? Not only alive but safe?" A soft squeak of delight escapes her lips.

I smile even more now that we're getting somewhere. I look back for confirmation from my partner and he nods, handing me the knife blade first. I take the steel in my hands, turning it around so that way the handle in in my palm.

"Don't make me use this Camilia," I threaten, using her name for the first time, running the metal against her bare throat. It catches a piece of skin and makes a small cut, a tiny hiss escapes between her teeth. "All you have to do is tell me what I want to know. I know that you've been through a great deal of pain. Agreed?"

"Yes," She barely squeaks, great shame emanating from her.

I turn around and survey the white, blood stained room real quick. My eyes catch hold of a chair and Bryan brings it to me so that I may sit.

"What's your full name?" I start out with.

The question is so simple and easy, yet I can tell there's a deep struggle within her on telling me. She's been sworn to secrecy, one that requires her not to tell me anything; although, the rebels do not require their followers to take the information to their graves before releasing anything like we require our soldiers.

"Camilia Reyes-Alejandro," She states her full name.

"You're married then. To whom?"

"Sebastian Alejandro."

I almost drop the knife I'm so shocked, although no one behind the glass would know why. I wasn't expecting to hear a name that I recognized. That means she could be married to the boy Jason claims is my cousin.

"And your citizenry status?" I ask, my voice now coming out as squeaky as hers.

"Infinitive," She answers, almost ashamed.

"I'm assuming you're both rebels?" She nods as I attempt to clear my throat. "Then you would obviously know where your headquarters are," She nods again, ashamed. "Tell me," I growl at her, now trying to make it obvious that I'm in charge here.

She starts bawling again so I hand the knife back to Bryan just in case.

"I can't," She sobs.

One small nod from me and Bryan advances on her. In one second the knife is down by his side, the next it's up and cutting a slash through her eye. Instantly I stand, toppling the chair back as I march towards her. With one yank of my arm, she's slanted with her arm bent at an awful angle. My hand still holding onto the bar that keeps her suspended up above the ground.

"Lets try something easier," I snap, my voice has now completely lost any sweetness that it previously had. "Give me the name of another one of your leaders names. One who is not dead."

"I can't," She once again cries, blood mixing with her tears.

A cry of frustration escapes through my clenched teeth and I release my hold on the bar. It swings up sharply with ignerta, smacking into the ceiling, tossing her sideways. Bryan is also so frustrated that he slashes through her eye again, making it unlikely that she'll ever see again.

"I can't because I don't know," I reach out and grab hold of Bryan's arm; to stop him in case he tries to her so she can't speak. "Our organization is very private. The only reason I know who they were was because they are family," She says over to the noise of her blood plinking to the floor.

This once again baffles me. How can such an alliance have so many followers if many of them don't know their leaders?

"How can this be?"

She sucks in a breath, blood falling into her open lips before saying, "Many of us don't know any of our leaders. We are spread all over the country reporting back to our superiors. Who report back to their superiors who then report back to our leaders. They could walk amongst us and most of us would know who a single one of them."

I think about this for a second before saying, "So your leaders just let their followers sacrifice for them while they sit up in their comfortable offices."

"No," She says as if I've offended her. "Most of them are out there fighting and only come back when decisions need to be made. Several have died. Only then do a few get the privilege of seeing who they are."

This idea still doesn't make sense to me. I highly doubt that their leaders are out in the streets fighting our soldiers.

"So your leaders do come back to your headquarters after being gone?" She nods sobbing. "So then if you know two of your leaders then you know where your headquarters are. Tell us and we'll get you to see Jason."

Her cries grow louder now that I've offered some sort of reward for her compliance. "I can't. I'm sworn to protect them at all costs."

My venomous smile once again returns as an evil frustration builds up in me that I know will soon boil over.

"Sworn or not. I always get what I want."

I turn towards the door and leave while Bryan stays behind to try and properly scare her into giving us some answers.

Chapter Sixteen

Bryan and I are once again ushered into cars as we leave the pentertary but this time Bryan had a car to himself. When Ingram helped me into the car he slid in beside me. Now I sit staring out at Sleisia's capital with our countries royalty.

"That's where your family is buried, right?" Ingram asks, pointing out a passing soldiers graveyard.

Frankly, I don't know but I don't want to sound stupid in front of our Emperor so I say, "Right." Ingram stares at me with a soft smile and I can't help but wonder why I'm here. "I hope you don't mind me asking sir, but I don't get why I'm here. I could easily have ridden with Bryan, we didn't kill each other on our way over."

His smile widens even further and he reaches out to grab my hand that lays on the cool, black leather seats. He holds my hand between his two warm ones, gently caressing the back of my hand with his thumb.

"I have a little proposition for you, or an alliance if those terms are more common to you," There's a lump in my throat now due to nervousness. "As you well know, as soon as new royalty takes office we are expected to wed within a year," By now my heart is racing fast. "You are a very powerful, smart, cunning, attractive woman, Kiera. Things that are all desirable when it comes to royalty."

My heart races, he's talking about my traits being desirable for a royal bloodline.

"I've always thought you to be attractive. Someone who would look good by my side," He's talking but I'm afraid that I may be so overwhelmed right now that I might miss something. "I'd like you to stay by my side for the rest of my days. Be my empress. True that there is no love between us today but I believe that someday there could be."

My eyes widen as Ingram lets go of my hand with one of his, pulling out a box from his pocket. He officially drops my hand so that way he may open the velvet, black box. Inside rests a silver band that holds an oval shaped stone. A deep blue (the same ones as our country's colors) stone rests at the very center of the ring with several smaller diamonds around it. My pointer finger reaches out and gently touches the pretty jewels.

"Do you, Kiera, promise yourself to me, your emperor? Not only as a companion but as a friend, lover and confident," He now holds my hands and ring, poised to slide it onto my finger.

"I do," I'm barely able to say.

With one single push he slides the ring onto my left hand. It amazes me that it fits just perfectly. The ring looks like it was made for my fingers; the bigger centerpiece makes my fingers look small and delicate.

"This ring has been worn by every empress who has sat on the throne for the past three-hundred years," He says and I can't help but stare down at the vulnerable, ancient thing that is now mine.

He stares down at my face for a long moment before saying, "I hope you don't mind if I try something."

I shake my head; as if I'd ever tell the emperor no. Ingram starts to lean towards me and as soon as his eyes slide shut, mine do as well. He presses a soft kiss to my lips, almost as soft as when he kissed my hand. The kiss is very nice, it leads me to want another, it brings me to believe that there could be real promise with us being together. When he pulls away I sigh slightly, that was a good kiss. We both stay leaned back against the seat, breathing in a bit. Right now my brain is over analyzing what just happened.

I clear my throat a bit before deciding to say, "I assume that we have some sort of a back story that will be presented to the public."

For someone who just did something very serious he has the greatest of ease laughing. "You're very blunt aren't you?" I kind of shrug my shoulders in response which makes him laugh even more. "The story is that we've been together since before my father passed away. We are only just now announcing our engagement because it's time for me to marry." I nod along as he paints the picture of our story. "We can fabricate the pictures and release them at some point as proof that we've been together for a long time."

My mind is cleaning up from the shock of the new and I analyze the details of the arrangement. The more I think about it, the less flattered I feel. He clearly needs someone strong and commanding, a person who could hold her thumb over his military. A woman who looks good beside him, but if danger strikes knows what to do. Sure he needs a companion, but what he wants is someone who could handle the whole country if things went badly. If anything, he'll probably hope that I don't care in the slightest if he goes off with other girls. What he wants is to combine my abilities with his strong bloodline to create a nearly invincible offspring.

For the rest of our ride Ingram jabbers beside me, feeding me details of our engagement. Apparently he has to publicly propose to me in front of the whole country. It does make sense why though, it's sort of getting a symbolic approval of me in front of the whole country. Our car pulls to a stop in front of some massive gates and I can just now see bits and pieces of the Emperor's palace. The crowd is a little daunting, especially when Ingram tells me that the volume of people will only be growing. The driver pulls to a stop directly in front of the steps. The palace is absolutely massive, with more windows then I could count. A hand is reached inside and offered to me; for one second I think about ignoring it but I have to remind myself that that isn't a thing that royalty would do. The new hand catches hold of my gloved one, pulling me out. As soon as my feet step outside the brisk cold slams hard against my face. I came out the right side, facing the palace, forcing Ingram to walk all the way around the dark vehicle so that way he may be beside me. Bryan pulls up behind us but no one offers to help him out. Once he joins us Ingram takes my arm, guiding me up the stairs. Bryan follows close behind us, cameras capturing our every step.

The wide, grand doors are opened for us, warmth guiding is in and the foyer is nothing like Ive seen before. The doors open up directly into the throne room. Creamy marble tiles guide directly back to two ornate thrones. Up above them is a huge tapestry of angles and a bunch of sunlight, something that is almost too beautiful to look at. The walls are decorated in a deep, velvety blue fabric that holds portraits of every past monarch of Slesia for the past four-hundred years. Through all the grandeur my eyes keep coming back to rest on the two thrones. There should be only one right now.

"Would you like to sit in them?" Ingram asks, following my eyeline.

I turn around, my mouth open, about ready to tell him he's crazy but then I remember that cameras followed us inside. So I smile instead, I nod my head ever so slightly. Ingram moves to clutch my hand and pulls me along behind him. Both of us giggle slightly, I feel beyond ridiculous but to the cameras watching us, we must look like we are head over heels in love. And that's what we need. Ingram spins me around and guides me gently down onto the throne cushions. The padding squishes slightly but still stays firm beneath me. There's cushioning along the back that feels rather nice and the entire frame is made of gold. Jewels adorn the top most part of the chair, giving the piece of furniture even more sparkle. My new fiancé takes the seat beside me.

As soon as he sits down, I can tell that I am seated in the more feminine throne. Both are just as ornate, but mine sits slightly lower than Ingram's. It's a bit more petite and it just makes me look small. While I do enjoy sitting in a chair that will soon be mine, I can't help but have my eyes flick back to the cameras.

Ingram sees me watching them and grabs my chin, turning my head so that my attention is back on him. "They'll just be getting a few pictures to make our story more believable."

The camera crew seems to hear their cue and they scurry over, not as thrilled to be close to us as I thought.

"If you could place your hand, Victor, ma'am, on his majesty's chest," One of the men holding a camera requests.

I take my now degloved left hand and place it on Ingram's chest so that the cameras can catch the slight sparkle on my finger. We are told to look at each other and smile. It shouldn't be that hard for me but it is. Ingram seems to be a perfectly nice guy but it feels wrong to me. A few pictures are taken of us then Ingram is directed to stand behind me. With one hand on my shoulder and the other on the back of the throne, both of us not smiling. All I can think about if the fact that these pictures will soon be plastered all over the whole country. As soon as we finish I lock eyes with Bryan, we both know how stupid this whole thing is. These men are dismissed and Ingram pulls me up out of the chair. He beckons Bryan over and leads both of us towards the wall, pushing onto it until a door is revealed. We walk through the door and the hallway we find is just as grand as the throne room. Long cherry wood floors, picture covered walls of giant murals that depict several different versions of the seasons. Bryan and I get a long tour of the palace that is soon to be my home. Chandeliers sparkle all over the place, priceless paintings, crystal everywhere, and grand ball tools that could fit hundreds of people inside.

"There are a total of ten libraries," Ingram turns around to smile at me. A while back we ditched Bryan after Ingram told him that we'll be going over things meant for only the ears of royalty. "But only eight are known about by staff except for a select trusted few, myself and now you, know about the other two as well. Those two libraries are for our own use only and any others that may come after us."

"What do those libraries hold?" I ask as we step onto the floor meant for royalty alone.

We walk along for a second, my arm through his, my heels not making any noise on the plush carpet.

"Any and every secret that our country has to offer," He says with a boyish grin.

The thought of so many unknown secrets not far from my grasp makes me slightly giddy. "May I see?" When I ask, my voice doesn't sound like my own.

Ingram laughs at my excitement. "You have a lifetime to go through it, darling."

I should be slightly concerned about why he shot down me seeing the library, but my stupid brain is too preoccupied by the fact that he called me darling. He leads me down the hallway pointing out different doors on our way. A family parlor, an empresses sitting room that I get to peek inside (the whole thing, while extravagant, is too frilly for my taste). He shows me different bedrooms, a nursery, then we get to the emperor and empress suite. The whole thing is decorated somewhat masculinely, exactly to a man's taste. Everything's rather dark, the bed is huge (giant four poster), a blue rug, a table that looks like it should be in a family's kitchen but is instead used to house different books and papers. There are several doors that lead off to I don't know what but I'm guessing one at least has to lead to a bathroom and another to a closet.

"I know that the decoration may not be to your liking but we can have it redecorated to accommodate both of us."

I smile slightly trying to seem a tiny bit less menacing then I usually do. I move and go to sit on the bed and it feels even better than the throne downstairs. My gaze rests on him and he watches me back. I pat the bed beside me, expecting him to sit but he just stares at me. There's a soft knock at the door and Ingram almost sighs in relief.

"Come in," He says just as a young servant enters.

"You have a visit in your office, sir," the young boy almost trembles with fear.

It's almost like he was just hoping that someone would come to get him.

"I have some work to get done," He says backing out the door slowly.

Soon he leaves me on my own and I'm left to my own devices. When I'm really sure he's gone I move over to the table with all the papers and books on the table. I sit down right in the middle of it all, slightly daunted by the sheer sight of it. Everything on the table was to much for me to sift through.

Dozens of letters lay there; letters from different people of the military, letters from the jail (those letters were about me and the other Victors), and a final one from a Sebastian Alejandro. The man who is supposedly my cousin has been corresponding with my own fiancé. I pick up the letter and open the envelope, not at all not at all feeling that I'm intruding. The top is addressed to Ingram.

Ingram,

Christian has just informed me of your soldiers once again requesting to be promoted another level. Need I remind you again? You cannot simply be promoted just by your request. I have so far done everything that you have asked by me. What more do I have to do? I willingly have positioned an anonymiss spot for your soldiers in our resistance so that way you can abort any small tasks that we may set for them but you have to be patient and wait through the line of promotion. Right now you need to focus on getting your military's full loyalty. Just because you know who our leaders are does not mean that you are one of them. Let me do my job.

Sebastian

I set the letter down, slowly and carefully back into the spot that I found it. So the man that I am engaged to has a spot in the resistance only so that he can control one of my relatives. I don't know if he's ordering him around or if Sebastian's willing working by his side. My hands scramble through all of the papers on the desk, trying to find something else, anything else. Finally, I come across Sebastian's latest letter. It reads…

Ingram

As you know by now, Kiera has worked her way up through the army. Use that power to secure your military. Don't hurt her. Please.

No name is signed at the bottom but I know it's got to be from Sebastian. The handwriting is identical to the first letter. I shuffle through the mess some more, trying to find anything at all. Then I come across a letter addressed to Sebastian from Ingram.

Sebastian,

I write to you now to tell you that I have got a solution. By this time next week I'll be engaged to Kiera. You may have been right when you said that getting her help might help me gain my army's loyalty. Within no time I could have the whole military if I have her as the Commander. Though, I have found out some information about her that you still have yet to give me. It's rather interesting that your cousin should somehow end up in my army. Your cousin who is soon to be my wife. Meaning that we are soon to be family. And family is supposed to help each other out. Not to mention that Kieranna Alejandro (once commander of the rebellion) has disappeared and I can't help but think of how similar Kieranna sounds to Kiera Anne. Meaning that I will soon be married to a lost, but still, commander of the rebellion. It would be awfully embarrassing for my wife to be higher up in the rebellion than for me to be. But then again, it's not like I couldn't just use what power she would have. Even now something awful has happened to her. Something awful that I intend to put a stop to with her help. As it turns out, there's a doctor out there who experimented on her by replacing her memories with someone else's. This whole mess is going to be terribly hard to take care of but you won't be here to do it, I will be. But I still can't help but think of how unloyal my messenger must be if he can't even tell me this information about my own fiancé.

Tears fall down my cheeks as I read the unfinished letter. I place both of my palms on either side of my head, towards the back, pressing hard. My sobs are choking me as I search my whole head. Sure enough there's a jagged scar on the back of my head. A line so thin that it wouldn't be noticed if you didn't know it was there. Someone else's brain is living inside my head. The thought completely terrifies me. Having someone else live inside me, it's absolutely revolting. I'm crying so heavily now that it's a shock no one has heard me and come in. My disgust grows to be so strong that I rush to the bathroom and empty my stomach with a few heaves. The smell is so strong that I think I may get sick again. I am forced to leave so that I won't vomit up any more of my lunch. I get back into the bedroom and I can't help but rest my eyes n the table full of papers.

My fingers comb through the piles greedily, making an even bigger mess if that is possible. I snatch up handful after handful of papers. Shoving them in my pockets, my waist band, under my bra, so that I may be able to finally look through them later on. A soft knock interprets me though and my hands grow still on the pages.

"It's open," I squeak, retracting my hands.

The door opens and Bryan enters, I let loose a breath that I wasn't aware I was holding. He eyes me rather quizzically and I must force myself to take a few steps back.

"I was sent to get you," Bryan says as he walks into the room. "It's time to announce your engagement."

"Ahh," I breath, making sure to keep my gaze on him.

He looks around the place before asking, "What have you been doing in here?"

I put my most fake smile on and say, "Royalty business. Things that you would never understand."

Bryan chuckles slightly and grabs hold of my shoulder as I get close to him, so that he can steer me outside the door. As we leave, I feel the pages burning into my skin.

Chapter Seventeen

That night I am placed in a different room to sleep; a different room from all of the papers. The papers that now lay in my suitcase at the bottom of the bed. Now I lay in bed dreaming of the girl that I interrogated a few hours ago. The memory takes me to a place that I have yet to see. A room stacked with various weaponry, crates stack sky high, and in the middle, a girl handcuffed and gagged, just looking at me wide eyed. I stare back at her, Camilia, not really caring to go untie her. It feels like I have to force my feet out of a mound of glue before I go to her. My knees crackle slightly as I crouch down to free her from her bonds but I undo it. Her gag too. As soon as I am finished she throws her arms around me, but I refuse to let my body hug her back. The feeling of betrayal courses throughout me.

"Thank you, Kieranna," She says just before my air supplies is cut off.

My eyes fly open to find that it is not part of my dream and there actually is a hand pressed to my nose and mouth. I jerk my body and try to fight off my attackers as best as I can but at least two people hold me down while a third keeps their hand pressed to my face.The man's palm stinks of sand and I struggle to suck in enough air.

"Stop it," One of them says from beside me. "We need her alive so she can talk to us and we can't do that if you suffocate her."

The man removes his hand from my mouth and climbs off of me. I suck in a deep breath, grateful to no longer have to breath in the sand smell. It takes a lot of force but I will my body go still. I go so still that both of the men that have a hold of me let go. I stay still for a solid minute, letting my hand go inch by inch underneath my pillow. The handle to my knife rests comfortably in my hand while the trio stands not too far from where I lay, discussing the fact that my skills aren't what they're supposed to be. Immediately after, I swing my legs out of the bed and grab hold of the man closest to me. The blade that is in my hand is pressed to the man's throat as I hold him to me. His two companions run towards him but I press my blade deeper into his throat in warning.

"Ah ah ah," I warn them. "Don't come any closer. What are you doing in my room?"

"We come from the rebellion," One of the men say with his hands up in front of him.

The man in front of me narrows his eyes slightly and my hostage kicks his heel back into my left knee. Instantly my knees buckle, the knife escaping my grasp when I hit the floor. My hostage immediately snatches my hands, pinning them behind my back. One of the other two men grab my weapon so that I can't make a grab for it. This time the three of them have the good sense to search me for any weapons. They don't find any more though; as if I could hide any in my little shorts sleep set.

"As I said, we're from the rebellion. Sebastian sent us," The first man says.

I try not to let my emotions betray me but my face reflect what I'm thinking. A slight grin is exchanged between my intruders.

"He needs you to steal something and bring it to him," The same man says, crouching down in front of me.

I can't help but roll my eyes, this man has made a critical mistake. You never want to be on the same level as your prisoner; you always want to tower over them, making them feel small and powerless so that way they won't fight back.

"Can't help you," I say rather snarky. "I'm a soldier. Not a thief. You've got the wrong person. Go try a prison. Not a palace."

The three boneheads laugh as if I've said something funny. "No, no, Ms. Kieranna, we need you."

A small growl forms in the back of my throat. "What do you need me to steal?"

"Don't think of it as stealing if the person you're taking will go voluntarily," The same man grins.

I can't help but flutter my eyes in exhaustion. "Kidnapping? Great!" I muster up as much sarcasm as I can for two in the morning.

All three of them laugh at the same time. "Slesia has it's soldiers kidnap people for them all the time. This should be nothing new."

I roll my eyes at how ridiculous my captures are but my knees are starting to hurt from kneeling on the carpet and I'm getting fed up.

"This is cute and everything but why can't you tell me who it is you want me to kidnap so that way I can call security and then go back to sleep."

The three of them grow silent. "Jason," The second guy says frankly. "We need him back."

And now for the first time I truly consider kidnapping a prisoner for them. "He's in the most heavily guarded prison in the world. It'd never work."

"We have a whole plan worked out. All you have to do is execute it."

I clench and unclench my jaw before saying, "But if your plan doesn't work, Jason will be killed and I will be thrown in prison. And there goes two of the leaders of your rebellion," I say with a chuckle, feeling small thrill to acknowledge that fact out loud.

The two in front of me let their eyes widen ever so slightly. Apparently that wasn't a fact that I should know.

"If we let you go, will you attack us?" One of them has the idiocy to ask.

I roll my eyes at them Of course I will attack them if they let me go. The idiot behind me even loosens his grip on my wrists. I could easily escape his hold now if I wanted to but I'm too curious now.

"How do I make this work?" I ask, confused how their whole plan is supposed to work.

"You won't be able to do this alone. But we can get you the written plans tomorrow," Immediately I think of having Bryan as my accomplice.

"What happens if I say no?" I ask, knowing that there is no way they'd let me go if I refuse.

"In that case, we'd be forced to reveal to the whole country that you are a leader of the rebellion and that you admitted it to us. And since you are not yet married to Ingram, there is nothing he could do to pardon you. Even if he did love you."

Ouch, low blow. The thug in front of me makes me think that I have no other option but there is no guarantee that he won't betray me in the end.

"I'm in," I say without any more consideration.

They all grin and I hate it. "We'll get a message to you tomorrow," he says moving towards me. "I'm sorry about this," he says before I am hit over the head and I lose consciousness.

I wake in my bed with a painful headache, one that I am quickly becoming accustomed to. All day I wait for someone to stop me but I'm even more anxious about someone catching me being apart of illegal activities. All through breakfast I wait and I wait for someone to come arrest me and when I get in the car to go back to my interrogation. Ingram rides with me so he can once again watch my work, although this time I assume he watches me for a different purpose. Ingram jabbers on beside me, talking about meaningless things, until I tell him that he has to be quiet so that I can prepare. Bryan walks the length of the hallway with me before it is time for Camilia's interrogation. The whole time I'm itching to tell him about my encounter just so I can tell someone. The time to enter her cell comes and I realize that I did not give the interrogation a single thought. I follow

Bryan inside the room and I find the girl is once again strapped to a chair. I'm slightly disgruntled that someone moved her from her hanging position. With one stern look and a flick from my wrist, she is being wrestled into her perch.

"Great," The prisoner groans as her wrists are strapped to the bar. "You two are back."

I laugh and can't help to admire her cheek though she is experiencing hives of pain.

"Jason?" She suddenly asks and for a second I think this may be the message the rebels are sending me.

But I think better of it. There's no way they would so stupid as to do it this bluntly.

"No," My heels click as I move towards her. "That's not how it works. I don't have what I want so you must fulfill your end of the bargain."

She does look much worse today, way too many cuts. I should remember to give Bryan a different weapon. Today I'm not going to play any games; she needs to start talking before I lose my patience.

"Let's pick up from where we left off," I say, grabbing my chair to sit. "Now tell me where your headquarters are."

"I can't," She whispers and I can tell that little defiance is a struggle for her.

I don't have to say anything, Bryan immediately goes to work. I notice that he still has his knife but today he uses the handle as a club. Her cries eventually become too loud for me and I have to tell him to stop.

"Enough Bryan," I snap just to make sure he hears me. "Now, Camilia, tell me what I want to know."

She briefly spits out a mouthful of blood and when she does I notice that Bryan knocked out one of her teeth.

"I only truly know the location of one," I can't help but groan in frustration when she says this. "I was blindfolded every time I was taken to any others."

"But you do know the location of one?" Bryan interjects, speaking for the first time.

She nods her head slightly and I get up from my chair so that way I wont miss a single word.

"It's in Oswana," She says and I can't help but gasp. "A basement in the Infinitive sector of Oswana. That's where I report back to my superiors."

"What was it that you reported back to your superiors?"

She directs her now blind eyes at me. "I was a spy. I spied on the military base there."

This girl is full of surprises. "There is no way that anyone is spying on our training center," I snap rather defensive.

Her head tilts to the side and laughs. In all honesty her laugh hurts me, it's like she's mocking me.

"There are dozens of spies in Oslia. Many of whom are playing as slaves within the compound. They are able to make it to the marketplace to our hideout and report at night."

There's a bustle in the hallway and Bryan looks back at me. "Kiera," He whispers with a jerk of his head.

I know what he means, people are struggling to get around so that they may get a message to our soldiers at Oslia.

"Kiera?" The girl asks from behind us.

For a second my panic rises inside of me. There is no way that she should be saying my name with such familitary.

"Kiera," She repeats, tonging my name. Then all of a sudden her whole body perks up. "Kieranna?!"

Her exclaim is so loud my heart nearly stops and I can tell that she surprises Bryan as well.

"Kiera," I snap at her.

"Kieranna," She says again and my heart continues to struggle. "How are you here?"

Shock fills me; this should not be happening to me. I open and close my mouth half a dozen times, unable to get any words out.

"Leave," Bryan hisses into my ear. "Before this gets any worse."

Bryan has to push me slightly to get me to leave. I struggle to walk upright but I am soon out the door, leaving the screaming girl with him. As soon as I'm out in the hallway I collapse back against the wall. Today could absolutely ruin me. Ingram rushes towards me and I worry that he's coming to take me away.

"Are you alright?" He asks, grabbing hold of my shoulders.

I have to blink my eyes several times before I finally believe that he is not here to take me away.

"Yeah. She was rather crazy, wasn't she?" I try to laugh to distract him from looking too far into it.

"She was," He looks back towards the door just as Bryan exits out of it.

He looks at both of us rather quizzically. "She won't be talking anymore."

Both of us nod, accepting it, and I can't help but slightly feel saddened. Ingram turns me around and directs both of us towards the door that will lead us out of the interrogation cells. Soon we are down in the lobby and someone brings me my coat. They help me put it on and Bryan once again places his hand on the small of my back, ushering me out towards the cars. Once again I'm trapped inside a car with Ingram.

"I thought that I should personally take you to your transport," He says, clutching my hand in his before letting go.

As soon as his touch leaves my skin I notice that my hands feel like little blocks of ice. I shove my hands into my coat pockets and have to bite my lips from yelping in surprise. My finger brush along a piece of folded paper; the rebels actually got me their plans. I play with it quietly, silently memorizing it's dimensions.

"I need you to do me a favor," Ingram suddenly commands me.

"Of course," I whisper in obedience.

"I have already sent papers to Sloeq Plan saying that you and Bryan have won. But someone of high authority must banish the other two. Since no one has a higher rank than you, in the military, I must ask you to be the one to do it," He all but pleads.

"Consider it done," I say without wavering. "That is if they haven't already deserted."

The car comes to a stop and I immediately get out, not waiting for him to say anything. Someone comes to help me out but I shove them away; for just one second I feel like myself. My bag is handed to me and I snatch it away.

"Until next time, my empress," Ingram says, coming to me and kissing my hand.

I let him finish before I pull my hand away. I am careful to keep my head bowed so that way he can't see my new agitation. Bryan is right behind me and I stalk away to the transport. Once were back inside I can't help but notice that we're in the type of transport that carries soldiers. Still all the same, a slave comes to take our coats and when she tries to take mine I stare down at her with my most menacing glare. She walks away with Bryan's coat as I shrug my grey coat closer to my body.We both sit and strap ourselves in as the transport starts to take off. I look out the window and notice that Ingram did not bother to watch us take off. He is long gone.

I wait a long while to take out the piece of paper, so long that Bryan has even dozed off. We are far from the capital and there is not another soul in the cabin (besides Bryan) when I take the paper out of my pocket. I unfold the paper gently, careful to make sure that no one is watching me and discover that it was actually written on stationary from the palace.

"Took you long enough," A garbled, sleepy voice says from beside me.

I sit straight up in my seat, slightly startled, crumbling the paper slightly. Bryan still has his eyes closed but I know that he was the one who spoke to me.

"You wrote this?" I stare down at the paper.

I slowly start noticing familiar things about the writing: the t's are to short and the y's are to sharp.

"Put it in your pocket too," He says without even opening his eyes.

I'm beyond baffled. "So you're a rebel?" I can't help but feel slightly disgusted at the thought even if I am suppose to be one.

"You could say that," He says with a groan, finally sitting up and opening his eyes. "But in a way you also couldn't. My allegiance lies with you. You are the utmost superior that I report to. I haven't been for the rebels in a long time. I started working again after I saw what they did to you. That's why it's taken me so long to do anything. I used to be your secret project."

My mind is struggling to take it all in. Apparently he never did truly hate me.

"You're risking an awful lot," I look down at the plans. "These aren't very detailed." I look over the plans some more and the things on here I could have come up with on my own. "Why do I need these if I have you coming with me?"

I turn the pages over to make sure that there isn't anything i missed.

"I don't know," He says matter of factly. "It was just what I was assigned."

Our transport eventually touches down in the desert and I throw my coat at the nearest slave, glad to able to shed it in the heat. As we exit the craft I feel as if our plans are burning a hole through my pocket. At any moment someone may be able to see that I'm a fugitive. As soon as we enter the compound, slaves scurry over to clear us of any sand. Her whole body trembles in fear, it's clear that the word of our winnings has spread. By the time that they're done, it's the quickest I've ever been cleaned. It goes without saying that Bryan and I both start marching off towards the commander's office where we know Christopher will be. A few soldiers follow after us, either assuming that we need back up or they were assigned to protect us. Bryan goes first and flings open the office door. When I go in behind him it's not really a surprise to see Chris sitting behind the desk and Lea sitting in front of him.

"Well, if it isn't the new Empress and her lap dog," Christopher exclaims like he's on the verge of being drunk; which he probably is. "What did it take to get the position, Kiera?" He's practically purring.

"Clearly something that you and your lazy ass never could," I growl, getting irritated to see him again.

"Congratulations," Lea says looking forward, almost like he's frightened. I simply nod in recognition, needing to get on with the job that I was assigned. "I'm sorry Lea," I can barely whisper before sucking in a deep breath, "As commanded by Emperor Ingram Derricks, you are both banished due to failing your training as Oslia soldiers and failing your country."

Surprisingly Chris starts to laugh uncontrollably while Lea stays facing forward, already accepting it.

"Take them away," Bryan barks at his soldiers.

They move and cuff them both. Lea hangs his head low in shame as he leaves but Chris has the nerve to stare us down.

"I'll see you soon," he almost threatens.

I make sure to shut the door hard behind him. Those two will go wait in a cell, stripped of everything but their clothing, Soon they'll be thrown into the back of a ground transport and driven out into the middle of the desert. They'll soon die or find shelter somewhere in our enemy's territory. With the door closed I an very careful to sit in front of the desk even if I'm higher ranking than Bryan in every aspect.

"So everything that Jason has told me so true?" I ask calmly after Bryan has taken his seat.

"As far as I can tell, yes," He folds his arms comfortably over his chest, looking far more content than I've ever seen him.

I nod, leaning back in my chair and closing my eyes. "So this isn't me?"

"No," He says almost ashamed and suddenly it's hard to breath. I squeeze my eyes shut even tighter. "Your name is Kieranna Maria Alejandro and you are twenty years old."

My mind flashes through all of the brief memories that my mind has shown me so far. The little boy, Metias, is my main concern.

"Do I really have a little brother?" Suddenly worrying about a person that I don't even know.

"Yes," He responded and my nerves are already shot. "You never told me much about yourself. So much of what I know about you I found out through your records after you were captured."

"I'm twenty-one," I suddenly say, looking up.

He looks down at his hands which are folded in his lap. "You're actually twenty. The girl whose memories you have is actually a year older then you so your brain thinks you're twenty-one."

I nod, tears stinging my eyes. "Was I always this big of a baby?" I try to laugh, it's better to gain a year than to lose one. "Was the surgery performed here?"

He nods his head and I can feel my heart completely collapse. I think of the Doctor and all of the horrible things he's done. It's hard to imagine a single one of them being performed on me.

"Is there any way to fix me?" I can't help but hope.

"No," he looks down at his hands. "Parts of that girls brain has replaced yours but I don't think that all of yours was taken out. I'm hoping that with time you'll be able to remember some of the long term things that are still inside you. That means that you may not be able to remember everything but someday you could remember some things."

Chapter Eighteen

It's been two days. Two days of me staying in my office. Two days of me and Bryan planning. One day until I'm expected to return to the capital. Thirty days until I am to marry Ingram. Three hours until I see Jason again. Three and a half hours until he escapes.

It's two forty-three in the morning. Seventeen more minutes until Bryan and I leave for the compound. The minutes tick by deathly slow. I lay in my bed, supposed to be sleeping, waiting for Bryan to come to my door to wake me. Finally the knock comes and I roll over, letting my already booted feet hit the floor. Tonight I wear my training clothes so that I am prepared if it's a fight on our way out. He waits for me outside, in my office, handing me a plethora of weaponry that I can hide all over my person. Both of us march straight to the compound, not hiding the fact that we're heading there at such a strange hour. When we get there no one is there to clean all of the sand away from us. We are able to head to the experimental ward without any interference. The lights are all out, the Doctor having long since gone to bed. It still irritates me that when it comes time to unlock the doors, I have no pass codes, even I am now the second highest ranking person in our country.

We take the stairs two at a time silently making our way down there. Even though we shut off the cameras to the surrounding cells, we don't turn on the lights. No need for the prisoners to see us. My night time visit is completely different from the first time that I was down here. Any prisoners that were awakened by our entry scurry back to the back of their cells, scared that we may be a drunk soldier down here come to take their frustration out on one of them. We eventually get down to the last cells and find a man laying face down in his filth with a steadily increasing pool of blood beside him.

"His hand," Bryan points out, disgust filing his voice.

My eyes travel over to where his left hand used to be. The man who just came to interrogate him seems to be more of a butcher than anything else. The past two days I have been selfishly dealing with my problems while Jason was down here dying from blood loss.

"Grab him," I am barely able to choke out.

I fumble with the keys at my side so that I can hand them to him.

Bryan snatches them from me and says, "I'll take care of this. You just do your part."

I nod and spin around to face the very last cell, but my eyes catch the giant grey door. Bryan previously explained to me that I was kept and interrogated in that room. My whole body itches to go in there. Suddenly there's a sharp stabbing in my brain and all I can see is that grey.

"Kieranna. Go," Bryan finally acknowledging who I am.

His command snaps me out of my head and I continue onto the last cell where a man sleeps on the cot there.

"Val!" I hiss sharply.

The now shaggy head pops up from the canvas and looks at me sleepily. His bare feet swing to the floor and comes to the cell's door.
"What do you want Kiera?" He doesn't even bother to hide his disappointment over seeing me again. "Come to see you dead fiancé?"

"He's not dead," I say a little too loudly. "You owe me Val. I discovered what happened to me and all of you kept it from me."

It seems like he shrinks back inside his skin before asking, "What do I have to do?"

From behind me I take out one of his old uniforms and toss it to him, along with a folded piece of paper. He takes the paper first, giving it a once over before reading it again in shock.

How is this possible?" He chokes, staring down at the handwritten pardon. "And you signed it as empress?"

His voice has gone particularly high in shock. While planning to extract Jason from the prison, we thought that it would be rather hard if both of us just disappeared. It took a lot of planning but we were able to get our hands on a couple executive orders; one that would pardon Val from all of his crimes and making him the acting head of Sloeq Plan in Bryan's absence. The only way that any of this could possibly hold up was if I signed it all as Empress.

"We don't have time for this. Get dressed," I urge him on.

Right away he starts to strip down and I turn away. As soon as he's done and I'm ready to unlock his cell, Bryan has finished. He tosses me the keys and I let Val out. The first thing he does is latch his arms around me and I can't help but notice how strong he smells of human feces. Thankfully he lets go quickly enough and I am able to turn around to see Jason flung over Bryan's shoulder. I rush to them and let my fingertips graze over him gently, stopping short of the bloody stump that was his hand.

"He needs stitches," Is all that I can think to order but I know that he needs more.

Without another word Bryan rushes up the stairs with me and Val not far behind him. The three of us rush to the door in the Doctor's experimental ward that leads to his chambers. I wait slightly off to the side when he comes to answer the door after Val knocks. With my gun in my right hand, I position it against his head as soon as he's through the doorway.

"Fix him," I practically growl in his ear.

Immediately his hands fly up in front of him in surrender. Val reaches out and wraps a hand around his collar so that way he can pull him out of his room. Once he's outside the room I let my eyes wonder inside and the first thing that my eyes are drawn to is a giant bed. A girl, younger than I am, lays tied to the borders that holds up the mattress. All around her naked body is sizes of pools of blood, some already dried. I recognize her as one of the Infinitive ward, that is supposed to rot away there.

"Val!" I whisper harshly.

The Doctor's head turns with him but I flick up my wrist so that my weapon is once again placed against his temple. Val's eyes and mouth both form giant O's in shock. Were both thinking the same thing. Rape. It's one thing to know young soldiers inflict it on slaves but it's another to witness the aftermath of a Doctor doing it. Bryan lays Jason down on one of the nearby tables and I must take my eyes away from the girl, thinking that it would be kind of me to kill her so she'd be put out of her misery. I must remind myself that is something that a woman named Kiera would do. The one who stole my body. I watch silently as the doctor prepares a line of blood in an I.V. and positions it into one of the vines in his arm. We all watch him work, keeping him under careful watch of our guns. I've long since given Val his own weapons and he takes particular care to seeing that the Doctor never leaves the barrel's close watch. Soon his stump and many other cuts that are sure to scar are sewn up.

"Is there nothing you can do to help him wake up?" Bryan surprisingly asks.

A maniacal grin forms on the doctors face and I know that whatever he's thinking can not be good.

"There is a new steroid that I've been working on. It should restore his consciousness and strength within a couple hours."

"No way," I snarl at the same time that Bryan says, "Do it."

"No!" I scream when Bryan nods at Val and he snatches me within his arms.

He holds me there against my will as the Doctor grabs a syringe from a drawer. The clear liquid is pouring into the I.V. and tears start to stream down my face in worry. I squirm and kick at Val, hating the that even though he has spent days in prison, he is still stronger than me. As soon as the liquid is in his system, Val lets me go. I can't help but fling myself down by Jason's healing body, feeling more like Kieranna than I ever have before. Within ten minutes his color is turning back to normal. I practically have to peel myself off when bryan announces that it's time to go. By the time we've reached the ground floor of the prison it is four sixteen in the morning. Any minute now more guards will be put on duty.

We took longer than we should have but we eventually make it to the ground transport where we had previously stashed a bag of food and bottles of water the day. Bryan hops into the front seat and we take off with Jason laying down in the back seats with me clinging to him from the floor. As we speed away from the compound I can't help but realize that I will never see this place again. We hit a bump in the sand and we are jostled around, I can't help but realize that one of my head aches is starting to form. Hours go by and I remember Val's sad face watching us as we drove off. Bryan drives us in the direction that he can only guess the rebel's hideout is, but too soon we run out of fuel. We are forced to leave the transport behind us. Luckily, we find some rope inside and tear the leather off of the seats and make a make a shift gurney to pull Jason around on.

We've only been out here an hour and Jason is due to wake up any minute when I start to feel dizzy. I'm able to make it a few more steps before the sides of my vision starts to blacken. My right foot steps in front of me, and both of my knees fall away. I fall behind so that I'm staring at Bryan's back and Jason's face.

"Kieranna!" Bryan exclaims, noticing my fall.

Upon hearing my name, I swear that Jason's eyes start to open.

"Jason," I whisper contently, falling forward, my tongue starting to feel the taste of the desert sand.

The End